Contents

Children's Children

First published in 2016 by
Liberties Press
140 Terenure Road North | Terenure | Dublin 6W
T: +353 (1) 405 5701 | W: libertiespress.com | E: info@libertiespress.com

Trade enquiries to Gill & Macmillan Distribution
Hume Avenue | Park West | Dublin 12
T: +353 (1) 500 9534 | F: +353 (1) 500 9595 | E: sales@gillmacmillan.ie

Distributed in the UK by
Turnaround Publisher Services
Unit 3 | Olympia Trading Estate | Coburg Road | London N22 6TZ
T: +44 (0) 20 8829 3000 | E: orders@turnaround-uk.com

Distributed in the United States by
Casemate-IPM | 1950 Lawrence Road | Havertown, PA 19083
T: +1 (610) 853-9131 | E: casemate@casematepublishers.com

ISBN: 978-1-910742-29-7
2 4 6 8 10 9 7 5 3 1

A CIP record for this title is available from the British Library.

Cover design by Liberties Press
Internal design by Liberties Press

The publishers gratefully acknowledge financial assistance from
the Arts Council of Northern Ireland.

*All characters in this book are fictitious, and any resemblance to
actual persons, living or dead, is purely coincidental.*

Children's Children

Short Stories

Jan Carson

To Aisling
with kind regards

JP.

LIB
ERT
IES

JHS. Summer School

July 2016

For the Ulster Hall, and all those who've called her home

On the floor at the great divide
with my shirt tucked in and my shoes untied.
—Sufjan Stevens, 'Casimir Pulaski Day'

1.

Larger Ladies

They were not as fat as she'd expected.

Of the ten in Sonja's care, only one was too big to stand. An extra-large bed had been borrowed from the bariatrics department at the Royal. Bariatrics, she'd learnt, was the type of medicine which specialised in making fat people thinner. When it arrived, the bed was almost as wide as it was long. It did not fit through the ward doors, so they were unscrewed and afterwards screwed back wonky. Now they made a noise like sliced cheese every time they opened. The special bed ate into the space between the beds on either side, so Sonja could only approach these patients sideways. Like a crab, she thought, which was a good comparison, for wasn't she always pinching at them with needles and the device used for measuring flab?

The other women were just a little overweight, what Sonja's mother would have called plump: size sixteens and eighteens sheathed in pale, satin pyjamas. The damp, green glow from their monitors reflected off them so that they seemed to float on their beds like luminous squid, or jellyfish suspended in a tank. Her father, who had been more comfortable with livestock, would have called them hefty, would have seen no such romance swelling between the folds of their childbearing hips.

But they were beautiful to Sonja in their every-day-different pyjamas: peach, lemon, lilac and baby's-breath pink, all the colours of the ice-cream spectrum. They smelt clean while they slept, like the inside of Boots, the chemist. In the morning, Sonja went home smelling of them, sometimes talc and sometimes lavender. No one on the bus noticed or, perhaps, because this was East Belfast, they noticed and said nothing. Sonja did not mind their fat, or the way it wobbled when the machines went off. Neither did she allow herself to laugh.

The most important thing was not to laugh, or to look at them with pity. This was easier to manage when she didn't know their names.

Here was one middle-aged lady sleeping in a hospital bed, and next to her, another. Who was to say they did not know each other in the outside world? Perhaps their husbands were business partners or their children attended the same private school. Perhaps they were even good friends and met once a week, at the nicer end of the Lisburn Road, for cappuccinos or manicures. The first lady might believe the second to be in Spain, holidaying, whilst the first claimed to be in Cornwall, visiting relatives. It was not beyond the realms of Northern Irish hospitality to imagine them exchanging small gifts before parting: a tin of fancy travel sweets or a tube of scented hand moisturiser. This same hospitality did not extend to truth sharing, especially those truths concerned with having, and retaining, a husband into middle age.

Now, here they were on Sonja's ward, two proud women in single beds shoved tight as a terraced row, two proud women who, in the outside world, would insist upon distance. The sort of women who drove two-seater sports cars and wore earplugs every time they stayed in a hotel, and whispered, guarding against the possibility of sound-bleed between rooms. Here they were now in unflattering positions: double chins doubling on the pillow, grey roots emerging along their scalp lines and shadows creeping across their upper lips like teenage boys. They were without make-up in this room, which is to say they were defenceless, and also without wigs and false nails and fake tans, without the corsets and girdles and hold-your-belly-in pants they never left home without. Which is also to say they were honest as they had not been since childhood.

Arranged tightly together, they could hear the dry rattle of sleep breath catching in their neighbour's nose, could hear individual teeth grinding and smell the briny stench of piss clouding in the next catheter bag over. Here, they were now, a whole herd of women more used to seeing each other on the *Tatler*'s society pages, sleeping and sleeping and never knowing whom they slept next to.

Dr Turner had explained everything to Sonja. 'They'll sleep for a month or so, under anaesthetic. While they sleep, their beds vibrate almost constantly. It's a very simple science. The vibrations make their muscles do the hard work so they don't have to. They wake up thinner. It's the equivalent of six months' hard slog at the gym, and they won't remember any of it.'

'And does the weight stay off?' she'd asked.

'Hopefully not,' Dr Turner replied. 'If it doesn't, they're usually back here within the year.'

It was hard not to look at the fat ladies with pity. Especially, first thing in the morning when the lights came up and there were thin lines of drool visible on their chins and pillows, like snail tracks, from all that shaking. It would be so easy to laugh at them. Many of the other nurses did, calling the ladies names which were not their real names, but funnier (Frog Face and Betty and Hairy Claire) and sometimes arranging their limbs to look like the arms and legs of disco dancers.

One evening, Sonja arrived to take over from the day nurse and the day nurse had dressed several of the fat ladies up with bedpans for hats. She was taking pictures of them on her mobile phone; snip, snip, snip, the flash went off like a series of discrete fireworks. Even asleep, the women flinched.

'What are you doing?' Sonja had asked. She was particularly annoyed about the special-bed lady, whose head was so big that the bedpan sat oddly on the edge of her temple like the peaked hat of an American GI.

'I won't show them to anyone, only my boyfriend,' the other girl replied, defensively.

'I don't care. You shouldn't have done it in the first place.'

'Why does it matter, Sonja? They don't know what we're doing to them.'

'That's exactly why it matters,' she snapped back, and stood over the day nurse while she deleted every one of the funny pictures.

The most important thing was not to look at the fat ladies with pity or laugh at them. Once she started laughing, Sonja knew she would not be able to stop.

At night, when the overhead lights went off and they were curled up on a spare bed, shapeless beneath his Spiderman blanket, Sonja told Dylan stories about the fat ladies. 'They are mermaids,' she would say. He'd ask why they were sleeping, why they were wearing pyjamas and why they were not thin like the *Little Mermaid* off his DVD. He'd just turned four and there were so many questions in him.

'These are wise, old mermaids,' Sonja would reply. 'They are not skinny like the *Little Mermaid*, who is really only a child. They are tired from many years of swimming in the ocean. They have come to Belfast to rest because this is a good place to be. They have swum here from Australia and China, America and Spain.'

'And Poland?' he'd ask. Sonja would nod. 'Of course from Poland.' The East Belfast pinch on his 'A's caught her in the gut every time, and made her question the wisdom of naming him Dylan. The local tongue was cruel. It scissored his name into such an ugly, stab of a word. At home she would have called him Karol after her father, but that was a girl's name here, and Sonja wanted the child to be just like the other children, who were called Curtis and Jordan and other words which only sounded right on television.

Every Saturday evening, she went over his hair with an electric razor. The other little boys on the estate kept their hair close, running the streets in tracksuits and fat trainers like a troupe of baby convicts. She wished to see Dylan included, but could not bear to let him out the front door. He was only four and still went to bed with a sucking blanket. Each Saturday night, the pink-white of his scalp, peeking through the stubble like a shocked marshmallow, made Sonja cry, but she did not stop cutting. The sound of the razor's hum was stronger than her sobs, and more determined.

She didn't want Dylan to catch her crying. He was the kind of child who always asked.

'Why are you crying again?'

'Why does it never stop raining?'

'Why do the policemen drive tanks?'

'Why do we not have a garden?'

'Where is my dad?' This was a question he had not yet thought to ask. It was only a matter of time; most likely the questions would begin in September, when he started school. Sonja wasn't sure what she'd say. She didn't know the answer herself, but wished to say, 'Don't worry, son. I'll get you one.' This was what she said every time Dylan asked for something she could give him by saving or self-denial.

The child was always asking.

'Mum,' he'd ask, when they were on their own in the quiet dark, 'why are all the ladies in Belfast so fat?' Sonja understood why he might think this. All the women on their street were large and leant against their front doors in slippers like individual Samsons bracing their homes against collapse. And, Mrs McMillen at the VG, where they bought their bread and milk, was as big as the unsunk *Titanic*. She kept her bosoms resting on the counter, partially eclipsing the *Telegraph*'s front page. And here he was, every other night, sleeping in a room full of lady whales. It was not the best way to bring up a child. Neither was it the worst, Sonja told herself. Occasionally she wrote this in letters to her mother, who was always asking why she did not move back to Poland.

'They're not fat, Dylan,' she'd say. 'Fat isn't a kind word. They're just a bit bigger than the ladies back home.' Which was a silly thing to say to the child, for Belfast was his home now, and it would be years before Sonja could save enough to take him back to Lodz, even for a holiday. Her mother had only seen Dylan in photographs. Her father had died of a heart attack while he was still swimming inside her. Such a thoughtless thing to say to the boy; she hoped he hadn't heard. Besides, there were fat people in Poland too.

A circle of tubby grandmas had hung, like Christmas lights or bunting, around the edge of Sonja's childhood. Interchangeable Elzbietas and Ludwikas in tie-at-the-waist aprons and head-scarves. They could be relied upon for hot food in mountains, tending the table as if it was some sort of altar and the gods were always hungry. They were fat as butter, these little women, and shaped like stacking dolls or the kind of hedgehogs who wear clothes in children's books, walking upright on two of their four feet. They were quite happy to be fat. In Poland, fat was what you got when the blessings caught up with you.

During her first week at the clinic, Dr Turner had taken Sonja aside and said quite firmly, 'Never use the word "fat" in front of the patients. If you have to call them anything, call them "larger ladies", please.'

She'd written this in her notebook so that he could see the words 'larger ladies' neatly printed. She wanted the doctor to understand that English was no longer her second language.

'And is it "larger gentlemen" for the male patients?' she'd asked.

Dr Turner had laughed then, exposing the whiteness of his teeth. They were like tiny fingernails lined along his gums. The taste of coffee came off him every time he opened his mouth, for he was the type of man who leaned too close to women when he spoke.

'We don't have "larger gentlemen", Sonja,' he'd said.

'Do they go to a different clinic?' she'd asked, confused.

'No, they don't have their own clinic. You've clearly not been in Belfast long enough to realise that we don't have fat men here. We have fat women, and we have rich husbands who'll pay to send them to places like this. But we don't have men with that sort of problem in this city.'

This was not true. Sonja knew it. There were plenty of fat men in Belfast: the kind who wore their weight evenly across their bodies, as if the extra flesh had been applied with a spatula, and the kind whose fat was more unbalanced, balling about their middle like it might on a heavily pregnant lady. Every other man she passed was carrying the equivalent of a honeydew melon.

Sonja thought of Dylan's father then, and the way his belly hung loose from the waist, slapping against her like a wet pillow every time they made love. When she'd sat behind him in a taxi, going to the shops or the pub, she'd been able to see three thick folds in the back of his neck. *You could store things in there*, she'd thought, *like pencils or loose change*. She'd never mentioned this to

Dylan's father. He hadn't considered himself fat, for he'd once been a bodybuilder.

Later, when she'd said to him, 'I want to keep this baby,' and he'd said, 'Well, I don't,' and ordered her a taxi to, 'wherever the hell you people go', Sonja could easily have called him a, 'fat bastard'. This would have been true and would have poked away at him like when an eyelash is in your eye and it will not blink itself out. She hadn't said anything though, because Dylan's father was bigger than her and sometimes had fists. There had been the baby to think about too. The idea of Dylan was already uncurling inside her. The next day, she'd sent him a letter which said, 'You are a selfish man,' and, 'I did not ever love you even when I said I did.' She'd signed it, 'Yours sincerely, Sonja.' This was the wrong way to end such a letter, but she'd been copying a template off the Internet and couldn't think how else to finish it.

Sonja had not heard from Dylan's father again. Neither had she tried to contact him, even when the baby was born and looked just like him about the eyes. Once she'd seen him, out the window of a bus, on the way to work. Dylan had been three at the time, old enough to understand the difference between fathers and men you pass in the street without noticing. She might have lifted him onto her knee then, and said, 'Do you see that man in the Liverpool top, outside the pub, smoking? That's your dad, so it is.' But she'd felt all of a sudden jealous for her child and turned his attention towards the opposite side of the road, where there was a crane and a small dog pissing against a bus shelter. She did not want there to be other people in his world.

'Just you and me, kiddo,' Sonja would say each night, as she tucked him in to the hospital bed, clinking his safety rails into position.

'Just me and you, Mum,' he'd reply, 'and all the mermaid ladies.'

The fat ladies buzzed in approval. Their beds were on a timer and went off at precisely eight each night, vibrating steadily through a three-hour cycle. Three hours on the treatment. Three hours off. It was necessary to keep this up for at least a month if a patient wished to leave the clinic thinner. None of the ladies ever left early, nor did they complain about the bruises. Asleep, they were incapable of registering discomfort. However, the thin lines running from one side of their monitor screens to the other sometimes rose or fell sharply as if words had failed them and electricity was their new language.

After a week on the ward, Sonja was able to read the peaks and troughs of their dreams. The process of translation was not unlike Morse code or, perhaps, geometry. She traced their dreams out for Dylan, leaving greased streaks on the glass where her finger had made the shape of a mountain range.

'This is what a fear looks like when you are dreaming,' she would say, pointing out the lowest dips.

'And what are the high bits, Mum?' he'd ask.

'Those are the shapes a good dream makes inside your head, son.'

Sometimes, before Dylan fell asleep, they made lists of those good things they wished to dream about. Sonja insisted upon specifics: tastes, funny incidents, memories of day trips they'd taken on the bus to Newcastle and Derry-stroke-Londonderry (which was Dylan's favourite place to say, on account of its length). Sonja was not surprised to discover all her good things were resting against his, like books balancing upright on a shelf. She could not remember how she'd been happy here before him.

When the green lines were lowest, the fat ladies cried out in their sleep or thrashed around their beds like fish, straining against the leather restraints. This was how the bruises began.

This was the noise of young sheep, or very old women collected together in a nursing home. Dylan could not stand it.

'Make it stop, Mum,' he'd say. 'It's too sad in here.' Then he'd make a tunnel, pulling the Spiderman blanket over his head and keening softly into the mattress. Sonja would place her hand on the hill of his back, feeling each sob run up her arm and down her neck like a pulse of pure, electric grief.

Later, when Dylan was asleep, she'd make her confession to one of the fat ladies, a different one every night. Sonja was not a Catholic. She wondered if perhaps she should have been, for she felt neat inside, and younger, each time she spat the truth out and left it curdling in a stranger's ear.

'I am a bad mother,' she'd whisper, leaning across the safety rails so the stale-paper smell of their hair caught at the back of her throat. 'I bring my son to work because there's no one else to look after him. I am sad that he is here in this room with all of you. It's not the right way to bring up a child. But I am not sad that there is no one else. I could find him a father if I tried. I am still young and I have not lost my figure. All the time, men look at me in shops and on the bus. I could easily find a father for Dylan, but I am selfish. I don't want to share my boy with anyone else.'

The bed rails vibrating against Sonja's arms left marks and were a comfort to her. It felt as if the room and all its fixed occupants were offering her absolution.

Occasionally, she sang over the machines, or tried to harmonise with them, songs from *Mary Poppins* and *The Jungle Book*. She'd learnt these in a clipped English accent, because this was how songs were sung on children's DVDs, and there was nothing else to watch in the flat. 'A spoonful of sugar makes the medicine go down' and, 'the bear necessities of life will come to you'; nonsense words in a dark room. The ladies settled when she sang, their lines evening out to form ribbons and almost flat roads. And Dylan slept more soundly beneath his Spiderman blanket. He was all knees and angles when he slept on the ward, like a creature ready to bolt. She was glad she could not see the cut of his dreams.

Sonja did not sleep. She moved between the aisles taking wrist pulses and pressing her temperature gun into the ear of each lady in turn. The gun made a clicking noise upon entry and a thin beep when it was time to withdraw. This felt wrong to her, like shooting a person who is already dead. Sometimes she forgot to sterilise the gun between shots. This was not good enough. Sonja was normally tight on procedures, more so than the day nurses, who did all their checks in the last ten minutes of a shift and forged the patients' notes with different coloured pens.

'If they paid me a decent wage, I might be a bit more bothered,' the day nurse told Sonja. 'My last job was in an old folks' home. I made twice as much, with better holidays and all I had to do was shovel porridge into them three times a day.'

This infuriated her. It was not so much the absence of compassion as the laziness which made her wish to pull at this girl's very straight hair and say, 'Someday you will make a terrible mother.' Sonja had always been the sort of person who enjoyed rules and, where there were no rules, would invent her own to keep the hours from falling idle.

A quick squirt of hand sanitiser between patients.

Disposable, rubber gloves for drip changes and emptying catheters.

Dylan, to bed, as soon as the eight o'clock cycle begins.

A chapter of *Pride and Prejudice*, read aloud, each evening at nine. (Sonja assumed that these were the kind of ladies who appreciated Austen for her manners and her well-planned dinner parties).

With rules and order, the night could feel four to five hours shorter than it actually was. Before the tiredness had a chance to sink its teeth in, it would already be breakfast time. As soon as the day nurse arrived, she could sling Dylan over her shoulder like a damp carpet and slip away from this place. Sonja did not like to stay a second longer than necessary. She used Dylan as an excuse to leave. It was not the child. It was the way the room changed when the day nurse arrived, or Dr Turner. The ceiling felt lower, as if the room was only big enough to bear Dylan and Sonja and the sleeping ladies. The air was too thick to breathe.

'All good?' the day nurse would ask.

'All good,' Sonja would reply, her coat already buttoned against the Belfast drizzle.

'I don't know how you stand it, Sonja. It'd really creep me out being locked up in the dark with these freaks.'

'I like it,' she'd reply. 'You can turn the lights on if it bothers you that much.'

None of the other nurses wanted the night shift. It was strange to be in a room so full of people and yet so empty. At first, the stillness had sat heavily with Sonja. She'd paced the alleyways between the beds, talking to herself reassuringly, as she might've done in the presence of a ghost. Later, she'd grown to crave the silence. Living in Belfast made her twitchy. There were noises everywhere: helicopters, sirens, young men swearing at each other sharply in the street. She was always bracing herself. There was constancy here in the dark: the fat ladies slept, the machines mumbled gently, and no one from the clinic ever came unannounced.

There was a line where the clinic ended and Sonja's room began. Dr Turner crossed it first thing each morning, with a notepad in one hand and, in the other, a coffee mug. He stayed no more than three minutes, and for the entire time, looked uncomfortable in a room without accessories of any kind.

Beyond the ward's doors were pot plants and uniformed nurses, pastel wallpaper, en-suite bathrooms, and the warm, vanilla smell of private healthcare. Each of the fat ladies had checked into this holy kingdom. They had looked upon it and pronounced it entirely suitable for a short visit. 'No different from a five-star hotel,' they'd said, and packed their genuine-leather suitcases accordingly.

In the clinic they were not averse to telling lies for their patients' good. In the clinic it was understood (though never explicitly conveyed to the larger ladies or their husbands) that interior design of such a high calibre would be wasted on the comatose. And so, after sedation, the larger ladies were wheeled into Sonja's room and locked up like surplus stock or holiday merchandise waiting to come back into season. This was sad and might even have felt wrong, if considered too closely.

The doctors and uniformed nursing staff preferred to avoid the fat room as much as possible. They liked to see themselves as the bookends, supporting either side of a patient's visit. This thought helped them not to feel like horrendous human beings each time they noticed the mountain of genuine-leather suitcases stacked in the corner of the staff room.

'How long do the "larger ladies" stay for?' Sonja had asked Dr Turner, during her second week at the clinic.

'How long's a piece of string,' he'd replied. Sonja understood what he meant and wondered, as she'd often wondered, why the people here could not tell anything straight, always had a softer way of saying something hard.

'Days, weeks, months, years?'

'Good God, no, Sonja. We couldn't have them here for years. All that shaking, their brains would be liquidised. Three months is about all the human body can stand with this sort of treatment. Even then there can be issues.'

'What sort of issues?'

'Oh, the usual side effects: back pain, migraines, psychological problems, nothing too severe. One lady told me she was still dreaming of earthquakes a full year after she'd left the clinic.'

All this, and the slight possibility of death, had been explained to the fat ladies during their preliminary appointments with Dr Turner. It was their choice to come to the clinic. They'd signed the paperwork for themselves. 'I agree to remain under sedation until my target weight of ten (or nine or eight and a half) stone has been reached.' Generally, they ignored the small print, signed their names and then wrote the date below. However, it was the husbands who drove them to the clinic and picked them up afterwards, in low-flying weekend cars. More often than not it was the husbands who supplied the pens for signing.

Sonja hated these husbands, though she'd never met any of them.

'What is wrong with the men in this country?' she'd written in a letter to her mother, who was only six months into her widowhood, and still grieving. 'They are always wanting their women to be someone else. They are never looking at themselves in the mirror.'

Her mother had written back, a week or so later, with news of the weather and her cousin who was getting married and, three short sentences in block capitals, worth paying attention to. 'HOW QUICKLY YOU FORGET, SONJA. AREN'T THE MEN IN POLAND JUST THE SAME? FIND YOURSELF A DECENT ONE AND SETTLE DOWN.'

Sonja had known her mother was right, that it was not geography but something more fundamental which made men one way and women another. But she'd ripped the letter into little squares and binned them anyway.

On the evening she'd arrived at the clinic to find herself in custody of her first 'larger gentleman', Sonja was confused. She'd phoned reception, asked to be put through to Dr Turner, and got his receptionist instead.

'I have a man in my room,' she'd said.

'You do indeed,' replied the receptionist. 'Mr McDowell, target weight thirteen stone. You'll probably have him for about six weeks, Sonja.'

'He doesn't belong here, with the women.'

'There's nowhere else to put him.'

'But Dr Turner said it would only be "larger ladies". There's no such thing as "larger gentlemen" in Belfast.' Even as she said this, Sonja glanced over at the new patient, at the button-up pyjama top straining to meet across his belly and the way his thighs were splayed out on the mattress like ham joints. She realised how ridiculous this must sound to the receptionist.

The machines began to vibrate. It was already eight. The sound of angry bees filled the room as the first cycle of the night lurched towards climax. Mr McDowell began to shudder along with the larger ladies, his jowls jiggling like set custard. Sonja had yet to do any of her routine checks.

'Listen,' she said, 'I understand that men get fat too. And, I even understand that some of them might actually want to do something about it, but they can't be treated in the same room as the ladies. They'd be so upset; they'd be mortified if they knew.'

'They're never going to know, are they?'

'You can't be sure they're not aware of things while they're sleeping.'

'Dr Turner's pretty sure they're dead to the world.'

'I don't like it.'

'You're not paid to like things, Sonja,' snapped the receptionist. 'Get on with it or start looking for a new job.' She hung up.

Sonja held the phone against her ear for a moment, trying to regain her composure as she listened to the angry hum of a dead line. After a minute or so she placed the phone back on its cradle. She had wished to say, 'This has nothing to do with the "larger ladies". This is all about me. I don't want a man in my room.' But this was not the sort of thing she could say to Dr Turner or even his receptionist. Sonja was still struggling to admit it to herself.

She looked up and across the darkened room. Dylan was sitting on the edge of the new patient's bed, staring at him as if he'd never seen a man before. Sonja wondered for a moment if the child had ever seen a man before – really seen, not just in passing. Of course, men featured in his cartoon DVDs – broad-chested heroes and weaselly villains, rendered in bold primary colours – and there were men they passed every day; some they knew by name, like Phil, the postman, and Trevor, who came to do their windows twice a year. But there were no male staff members at the day care facility Dylan occasionally attended (these days, people were hysterical about men hanging around children), and he didn't have a father or even a grandfather to learn from. Perhaps, this strange ghost of a man was the closest he'd ever come to the species.

Was this a failure on her part? Would the child grow up odd for lack of role models? Was she being selfish, keeping him all to herself in this lonely room? Sonja didn't particularly care. She had a hunger for her son that was too sharp to bear sharing with any-one else. She would not know how to say this to another person or explain it without sounding crazy, but sometimes she looked at Dylan sleeping like he was a thing she could actually eat.

'Look Mum,' he called softly from the other side of the room, 'a mermaid man. He's the biggest one we've ever had. Is he going to stay for a while?'

There was a hook in the child's voice, an echo of the way he sometimes said, 'Can I go out to play with the big boys?'

Sonja crossed the room in three soft strides, wrapped her

arms around her son and felt his bony shoulders fold into her chest. His pyjamas were just out of the wash and smelt of lavender and outdoors air. His little body jittered frantically in time with the bed. This was always funny to him, and he was smiling now, beaming up at her with his big brown eyes, like mirrors of her own.

'Come down from there, son,' she whispered. 'Leave the poor mermaid man to sleep.'

Dylan followed her without question, across the room, to a spare bed where Sonja lay down next to him and held him tightly against her when the ladies cried out. Dylan slept. Sonja did not sleep, because she was not allowed to sleep on the ward and couldn't have slept even if she'd tried. She lay straight beside him and knew that tomorrow there would be more questions about mermaid men, questions about where they came from and why there were no such creatures in his life. She would have to tell him lies.

They were not safe now, Sonja thought, not even here in this dark, dark room. The machines clicked on and another cycle began. The noise was like an itch you could not scratch yourself loose of. She would carry it with her out of this place and into the next. It was nothing she did not deserve.

2.

People in Glasshouses

When we were younger and had not yet moved to the city, my parents ran a garden centre. They sold plants for outside and plants for inside, compost and, during the months of November and December, Christmas items: mostly outdoor decorations and trees. Throughout the rest of the year they stored their Christmas stock in the coal shed with the other seasonal products: Easter bunnies and reusable harvest wreaths, picnic tables (both portable and permanent), and – stacked in the corner like demure dancing ladies – dozens of pastel-coloured parasols, still in their plastic.

Rarely did anyone buy a parasol. This was the 1980s and patio furniture was considered too exotic for a Northern Irish garden, a concept better suited to the Continent, like sangria or shorts or UHT milk. The parasols grew older with each year unsold. Their plastic wrappers clouded over and, for aesthetics' sake, were removed. Still they did not sell, even though, for a brief period, there was a craze for outdoor benches and the parasol situation looked a little more promising. After a few years of being displayed in the watery sun, they paled a uniform cream and could not be sold. My father threw them in the skip with the skeleton spines of that year's Christmas trees. It rained on the skip and the parasols were useless as umbrellas. They could not even keep the rain off themselves.

'You live and learn,' my father said. This was what he usually said when he'd made a mistake that could not be fixed or covered up.

The following year he tried his luck with paddling pools.

It was a scorcher of a summer. My father could not have known this, but he claimed a tip-off from a man who ran an ice-cream van out of Portballintrae. By the start of the Twelfth Fortnight, all but one of the paddling pools had been sold. The remaining pool had a dent and would not sell, even when reduced. After some significant pressure, my brother and I were permitted to keep the broken paddling pool.

'Because we're not getting away anywhere this summer,' my father said, which was strange to us, for we'd never been anywhere further than Newcastle, and even then, returned to the garden centre in time for dinner.

My brother and I dragged our paddling pool into the front garden, where the hedge afforded a small amount of privacy. Each morning we skimmed the surface for leaves and leaf-dwelling insects. It was worth the effort with a shrimping net for we were out from under our parents' gaze and also the curious glances of customers, who could not tell where the garden centre ended and our private world began.

We soon discovered a tiny tear in the pool's liner, no bigger than a buttonhole, where the metal side had pinched into the plastic. Sometimes we took turns pressing a thumb over the hole to stem the bleed of lukewarm water. This was a game to us, like splashing with saucepans or stirring up whirlpools with our arms. Most days we did not think about the way there was less water in the pool than there had been earlier in the day. We were six and four that summer and not yet aware that everything diminishes with time. In the morning we topped the water up with buckets.

We spent the entire summer outdoors, crawling in six-foot circles around the paddling pool's sides. Our parents did not think to apply sun cream. This was not just neglect on their part. No parent in Northern Ireland would think to apply sun cream until 1988 and, even then, only at the beach. It was too shallow in the pool for proper swimming or ever being underwater. So, we elbowed our way around the edges like creatures emerging from some primordial swamp. We had not yet grown legs. Our necks and shoulders, rising above the waterline, turned the colour of uncooked sausage, then burnt and peeled away in flakes like boiled potato skin, to reveal peach-gold flesh and freckles beneath. Our hair was the white-blond hair of children from American television programmes. At night, in bed, I held my face in the crook of my elbow. The smell of sun-blessed skin could almost be tasted and was a comfort to me. I could not explain why.

The next summer it rained and we couldn't find three dry days in a row to get the paddling pool out. My father had ordered six dozen more from the suppliers and did not shift a single unit. It had not been a good year for the strawberries either.

'We're leaking money,' my mother would announce each Saturday evening after she'd finished the books. *Like the paddling pool*, I'd think, and imagine a tiny tear in the fabric of the garden centre, in the polytunnel, most likely, and my mother stopping it with a dishcloth.

The A-Team was always on while my mother did the books. We'd be half-watching the television, my brother and I, half-listening to our parents argue as we ate our carry-out off our knees. When the argument had swollen to a point where it could not be contained within the walls of the kitchen dinette, my parents carried it outside to the greenhouse, where they could yell at each other without being heard.

My parents were fortunate to have a greenhouse in which to conduct their arguments. Other parents, I would learn from friends and early lovers, were forced to scream at each other on the hall landing with the door closed or, when concern for the children became an issue, take their arguments outside to the garden, where it was almost always raining.

We liked to watch our parents fight. They were more believable than *The A-Team* and did not pause for advertising breaks. We soon learnt to turn the kitchen lights out so they could not see our silhouettes watching through the sink window. They never touched each other but I could tell from the way they leant in to the anger, and drew back, which words were the very worst ones.

'Do you think they'll stop being married?' I'd ask my brother, and he always replied, 'Maybe someday, when we're older.'

He was seven then and wise enough to know when to tell the whole truth and when a smaller part of that same truth might suffice.

'Do you think they'll get rid of the garden centre?'

'No way.'

I believed him when he said this because he said it quickly, without elaboration, and it was the thing I most wanted to hear.

My parents had never intended to run a garden centre. My mother was trained to teach children in a primary school. She had not yet been able to do this for money, only for free, as a student. My father was a man who sold things at Nutts Corner market, and before that, a man who sold things round the doors, and once, briefly, a bartender, which was how he'd met my mother.

My mother often said to me, 'Life would've been much easier if I'd stayed in that night and never met your father.'

My father often said to me, 'It just so happened to be your mother. It could have been any wee lassie in a skirt.'

They should not have said these things to me. I checked with my brother, and they'd said similar things to him, and worse. He was older than me, and a boy, which went some way towards explaining why.

'Why do they hate each other so much?' I asked my brother, and he assured me that our parents did not hate each other, that this was just how adults got on when they were stuck running a garden centre they did not want.

Before the garden centre became a garden centre it had been a farm. The farm belonged to my grandfather who died. The day before my grandfather died, he'd asked to speak to my mother alone, in his hospital room. My mother was his only child. There had been a son. The son had also died. Something to do with a tractor, or perhaps a bull; the details were never discussed with us. It was assumed that my brother and I would know all these family stories, without being told.

In the room, alone with my mother, my grandfather said, 'I'm dying Susan, and I don't want this farm going out of the family. Promise me you'll keep it after I'm dead.'

My mother had loved her father. He was a good man, if somewhat quiet, and given to strong religion.

'Yes,' she'd said. 'Yes Daddy, I'll keep the farm on after you die. I promise.'

At the time she'd been crossing her fingers behind her back so my grandfather wouldn't see. Later, this would seem silly to her. She was twenty-three years old that summer and more than capable of breaking a promise, even with uncrossed fingers.

My mother did not want to have a farm. She could not stand the smell of sheep feed or the way it could not be washed out of clothes. She wanted to be a teacher of children in a primary

school, possibly in Belfast. My father, who was by then already
her husband, did not know what he really wanted. He was reasonably certain it wasn't a farm.

'Could we sell it and emigrate to Australia?' he'd asked. This
was on the morning after Granda's funeral. The hearse had not
been paid for yet, nor the dear, white flowers which covered the
coffin's lid during the service.

'No,' said my mother, her lips frosting around the edges. 'We
are not selling the farm. We are not emigrating to Australia.'
(Though she might have been persuaded if he'd waited a week
or so before asking.)

'You don't have to keep your promise to your dad. It was
unfair of him to ask.'

'We're keeping the farm,' said my mother. Once this was said,
she meant it. Even so, she could not picture the two of them together, with livestock and potatoes.

The garden centre had grown from the gap between my parents. It was not quite a farm. Neither was it a promise entirely
broken. The barns came down and the greenhouses glassed up
in their place. All the livestock went off to market in a neighbour's
truck and did not come back. Where the potato drills had been
there were soon polytunnels, sweating out strawberries and tomatoes like tight, red pool balls bunching on the vine. My mother
had plans for a coffee shop. The coffee shop never materialised
but she often mentioned it to her schoolteacher friends when
they called in for bedding plants or shrubs.

My brother and I were most easy amongst the plants.

We set our seasons against their seasons and grew accordingly.
In spring we shot forwards like bloom-faced sprouts, pencilling
our progress against the coal-shed door. In winter we were
underground creatures, dozing in front of the television, all our
green potential propagating beneath fleeced blankets and duvets.

Seeds we were, my brother and I, or small bulbs, always angling towards the sunlight.

We could not bear the feel of closed curtains or summertime spent indoors.

Neither could we imagine a house without a garden or, worse still, a paved backyard. The idea of an apartment was a sort of disability to us, perhaps as bad as blindness. We quietly pitied those children who did not have their own garden centres.

'What do children do if they don't have a garden?' we once asked my mother.

'They go to the park,' she replied.

We laughed at the ludicrousness of this, using the same made-up laughter we'd invented for Christmas-cracker jokes.

There were hundreds of places to hide on a garden centre, for example the polytunnels (which smelt of money, sweating) and the outhouses (which smelt of meat and leaves or, put simpler, compost in plastic sacks), the larger trees and the shed, where my father kept his tools and sometimes went to smoke when my mother was after him to do something around the house. The greenhouse was the only place on the garden centre no good for hiding. Even in summer, when the tomato plants were heaviest, you could be seen clearly through the glass, like a person lying beneath untroubled water.

My mother understood this. She was always sending my father to the greenhouse for tomatoes or watering or pricking the fledgling plants into individual pots. She liked to keep him behind glass as if he were one of the animals, stuffed and mounted at the Ulster Museum. Sometimes the glass was for holding him in and sometimes for keeping him out.

It was easy enough to tell which side of the glass my mother was standing on.

On the worst days, she did not get changed out of her bedroom clothes. She stood at the sink window, turning the same wet plate like a steering wheel, round and round, as she watched my father pace the greenhouse aisles with a can of bug spray. You could tell there were sore things she wished to say, but the language for this was stuck inside her and only her hands could move.

At other times, she'd take a mug of coffee out to him, on a tray with biscuits. She'd set it carefully on the potting bench, making room amidst his gloves and trowels. If she was wearing shoes instead of slippers, we'd know the coffee was only an excuse. She planned to stay and fight for an hour, or fifteen minutes, however long it took to empty her out. Afterwards she would cry, but never in front of us. Afterwards there would not be proper dinner, only toast or jam sandwiches, with yogurts for pudding. We did not particularly mind this. It felt like eating breakfast at the wrong time. This was a feeling not dissimilar to birthdays or when someone from the family was sick in hospital and anything was permissible.

'Why do they always fight in the greenhouse?' I asked my brother.

He did not know exactly, and tried to guess from all the television programmes we'd seen of adults fighting in England and America.

'I think it's so she doesn't shoot him,' he said.

'Because it's too dangerous to fire guns in a room made of glass?' I asked.

'No,' he replied, 'because everyone will see what she's doing.'

My father cheated. Not just with women, also in business and sports, and once on the transfer test between primary school and secondary. He was one of those men who could not content himself with happiness. He went at it like a raised scab. He smoked and did the lottery and stuck his fingers in the trifle for a lick before it set. If you asked him straight up about any of this he would say, 'Your head's cut,' or, 'You've the wrong end of the stick there, my friend,' or, quite simply, 'It wasn't me.'

It always was, yet my father had come to believe his own alibis. He would look genuinely confused by the lottery ticket gone through the wash in his trouser pocket, or the track marks in the trifle cream, or the girl from the next farm over with her six-month belly rounding up and her father on our doorstep, shouting, shouting, shouting through the letter box, 'I'll be back with my gun, you wee bollocks. You can't hide in there forever.'

'Cheating's easy,' he said to us, one evening, after drinking beer. 'Getting away with it's the difficult part.'

My mother was out at a church thing for ladies and could not hear him.

My father laughed when he said this – *ha, ha, ha* – as if he actually thought he was home and dry. This was the summer after the paddling pool. The grass had not yet grown back. On the front lawn a dead, yellow circle marked the place where our pool had been. The grass was swirled around on top of itself like the way a baby's hair will be on a hot day, after a nap. I was sitting on the arm of the sofa and could see the mark of it through the living room window, even as my father was saying, 'Cheating is easy.' Everything leaves marks, even water.

There were marks on the greenhouse where the compost bags had rubbed against the glass, leaving behind the idea of mould. The idea of mould became moss when filtered through warm glass and August rain. By the end of the summer the moss was everywhere, creeping up the windowpanes in bearded green waves. My brother and I amused ourselves with flat stones and trowels, easing a blade edge beneath the moss, peeling it off in inch-thick strips like unbroken slivers of sunburn. Beneath the mould the glass was stained the tea-strong colour of yesterday's piss. It would not clean off, even with spit. But it was still glass and more transparent than walls.

All summer we watched my parents in the greenhouse, taking their words out on each other. They closed the door behind them and thought themselves wise for taking this precaution. They became sepia-tinted in the dirty glass and this saddened me, because their clothes sat oddly against their antique faces, and were not stern enough by far.

My brother and I made portals in the greenhouse mould, lay belly flat on dry potato sacks and watched our parents like a cinema film. We could not tell for certain what they were arguing about. Probably the garden centre, which was still leaking, or the girl from the next farm over, who was fit to bursting now with the things my father had done to her.

'You stay in there,' my mother screamed at my father, 'in the greenhouse, where I can keep an eye on everything you do.'

She closed the door behind her. It slid from side to side and settled, like the door on a fitted wardrobe. If you pulled the door too hard it came right off its runner and could easily fall on you and shatter. You could die from this, like the man my father knew, from Portglenone, who'd tripped head-first through a patio door and severed a major artery. We were particularly careful when entering and leaving the greenhouse. My mother was not careful after a fight. She was slam and bang and 'Stay the hell out of my way, Richard!' in a voice you could have heard two fields over.

My father stayed exactly where my mother left him, in the greenhouse, for an hour or sometimes three. He pottered around the strawberry plants and did significant things with bamboo canes. It was difficult to tell if he'd intended to stay there, gardening, or was following my mother's instructions like a grounded child.

My mother watched him through the sink window, the lower

half of him invisible and possibly dishonest, where the moss had grown over. My father's face could easily be seen, also his hands and the part of him where his legs met his body. Every so often he lifted one of his visible hands and waved at my mother in the kitchen, as if to say, 'I know you're there, watching.' My mother did not wave back.

In the autumn, when the girl from the next farm came to our front door with a letter for money which my father would not pay, my mother said, 'Enough is enough.'

She put my father's pyjamas in a suitcase with a Bible and a toothbrush and she said, 'Enough is enough, Richard.'

My father did not say, 'Your head's cut,' or, 'You've the wrong end of the stick here, Susan,' or even, 'It wasn't me.' He looked like a parasol that would not sell.

That night he moved into the greenhouse. It was cold in there so he took a blanket and a torch for reading the Bible. He thought this might please my mother, on account of her father having been given to strong religion.

'I'm not leaving, Susan,' he said. 'I'm going to live in the greenhouse where you can watch everything I do until you believe that I am a different man now, a man you can trust.'

That night my brother and I watched him change from his day clothes into his pyjamas. In the moon dark, we could not see anything particularly naked about our father, only the whiteness of him, smudging against the black. He brushed his teeth in the outside tap and settled down to sleep with a compost bag for a pillow.

'What will the customers think?' I asked my brother.

No one we knew had a father who lived in a greenhouse and I did not want our family to become a story which people told at funerals and christening dinners.

'Wait and see,' said my brother.

He was almost eight then, and already old enough to understand that people did not function in the same way as kitchen appliances.

The next morning I woke early and my mother was not in her bedroom and she was not in the bathroom and she was not in the kitchen, fixing my cereal in a plastic bowl.

My mother was invisible to me, tucked behind the greenhouse moss. When she stood up, the body of her unfolded into view and I saw, from her hair (which was all spun and muddled), and her clothes (which were yesterday's, crumpled pyjamas), that she had been there all night, lying beside my father and the tomato plants. Afterwards she came out to us and said nothing of the greenhouse. We had jam sandwiches for breakfast and orange juice. The bread in my mouth would not chew itself down.

My father did not sleep in the greenhouse again.

My father cheated for fourteen years. There were also years before I knew him. My mother understood all this, and stayed. There were deep folds and hollows on her face where his lies had written things she could not wipe off. That summer I was not yet old enough to read by myself. Later, I would learn with books. Later still, I would look at photographs of my mother, taken during this period. It would be impossible not to see certain sentiments etched into the sad pitch of her eyebrows: 'I have failed and I am still failing,' 'I am basically OK with disappointment.'

I'd like to believe that I would have been a stronger woman in her shoes, but I have not yet been given a garden centre to contend with.

3.

Still

I was not always a human statue. After college, I was briefly and unsuccessfully a postman, then a traffic warden and, finally, a bus driver. By the age of twenty-six I had begun to find movement problematic. I liked to sit on benches and indoors on the sofa, not speaking, not even reading or watching television. I was quite well suited to buses, though the pleasure of being seated could not disguise the miles I moved every day, shuttling gun-faced commuters from one side of the city to the other. After a few months the wheels began to overwhelm me.

Karen said I was lazy; that I was nothing compared to the capable husbands of her friends and sisters, that she had not agreed to marry a slob. There were arguments around the kitchen table, some coiled, others as loose and loud as glass imploding. She signed me up for a six-month trial at the gym. I went once and, terrified by all those legs and arms pumping like fleshy pistons, never returned. I couldn't expect Karen to understand. It wasn't laziness which kept me seated, so much as a fear of overcomplicating things. There were so many necessary processes to concern myself with: thinking and breathing, heart-beating, hair-growing and fretting over the various problems we'd accumulated like warts and other crabby itches. I had no energy left for moving.

Over a period of several years, the stillness caught up with me and settled. It was a disease crawling up my legs and arms, across my ribcage, until even my heart could hold its breath, as if underwater, for a minute or more. It was a disease and I was all the better for believing in it. When the city council advertised for statues – first for the spring festival and later as semi-permanent fixtures – I was ready. This was the closest thing to a calling I'd ever had.

Karen wasn't so easily convinced. 'Think of the money,' I said. I could already picture myself paying the electricity bill in small-coin shrapnel and, if the punters proved generous, taking on the mortgage too. Eventually she agreed, but only if my costume was good enough to guarantee anonymity. 'I'd be mortified if anyone recognised you,' she said. 'I'd sooner they caught you having an affair.'

I have been a statue for five years now. I no longer move more than the necessary mile to work and back. I prefer public transport to the indignities of bicycles or walking, which require enormous amounts of concentration. At first I found the long stand something of a stretch and could not stomach the outside weather. However, I have, over the years grown accustomed to this, and also to the pigeons. Karen has not.

She tells her friends I work in a call centre on the edge of town. She asks me constantly, first thing in the morning and after we make love (slowly and deliberately, in a reclined position), why I couldn't take a job in a call centre. Karen does not understand that sitting down is not the same as stillness. I can't be angry with her. Very few people are called to be statues, and even fewer are cut out for marriage to a man who'd prefer to be made of concrete.

Most days I am Napoleon. Over the years, I have noticed that even uneducated people and teenagers will recognise Napoleon. The hand inside the jacket is a dead giveaway. Above all other possible statues, Napoleon suits me best. After a brief flirtation with Shakespeare, I settled upon him and stuck. I have the hat and the trousers, the jacket with its brass buttons running like typewriter keys across my belly, and a reasonably authentic sword Karen found at the Saturday-morning antiques market. Hand tucked like the man himself, I can hold my elbow at a forty-five degree angle for hours at a time. When the winter knuckles down, one hand, at least, remains reasonably warm.

Last December, when the water pipes froze and all the other statues stayed home for fear of exposure, Karen wouldn't let me out of the house without gloves.

'Napoleon didn't wear gloves,' I argued, and she snapped back like stretched rubber, insisting health and safety came before historical accuracy. In the end, I took the gloves just to please her, and kept them tucked inside my back pocket where the punters couldn't see them. Some things are better kept from Karen: things such as the gloves and the drunken football fan, who, mistaking me for a real statue, pissed against my shins, souring the leather on my handmade boots.

The stillness has also served me well in marriage. I am capable of holding my temper like a perfectly plumb line. I am capable of holding a secret for as long as it seems necessary. Karen does not know how lucky she is.

I am perfectly built for Napoleon: five-foot-six in my shoes, five-foot-ten if I stand on the plinth. The plinth brings me up to eye level with Sherlock Holmes and the moon-bellied Henry VIII, who share my High Street pitch, but I don't always carry it with me. The plinth is a nightmare to manage on the bus. It is roughly finished in plywood and catches on the sheer tights and stockings of those ladies busing to their office jobs on the other side of town. They glare at me through heavily lacquered fringes and roll their bruisey eyes as if to say, 'Do not touch me, do not look at me, do not think about the laddered plucks, delicate as spiders' steps, climbing the naked wall of my thigh.' They do not speak to me, and I cannot speak to them. The human statue must remain silent at all times, even on the bus home. But I think about them sometimes while standing still. I imagine them crossing and uncrossing their legs in air-conditioned offices, the ladders creeping up their shins, as slow and deliberate as the evening tide. I think about these stripe-suited ladies, and the thought of them is a warm fug catching between my costume and my white winter skin.

During the two warm weeks of summer, I am Julius Caesar, splendidly robed. It is good to feel the hot city air burrowing up my sleeves, the thin hairs on my arms rising and falling in fragile rebellion. The rest of me holds its silence like a state secret. I am proud on my plinth, and the punters cast their devotion around my feet in circling coppers and five-pence pieces. Even Karen says I look good with my grey flesh on show and my silvery hair pointed and prickling around my laurel wreath like uncooked meringue.

During the summer we make love in the evenings. I am Julius Caesar just off the bus, and Karen lays a dust sheet across the living room so my make-up doesn't come off on the carpet.

It is during one of these sessions, when I am balanced above her, barely moving, that we make the baby. I feel nothing. I am a cloud of myself, almost entirely removed from the situation. When we make love, I cast a still, grey shadow over my wife as if predicting the imminent possibility of rain. Karen immediately understands that everything has changed. When you are married to a human statue, the slightest movement is monumental.

'Things will have to be different now,' she announces, sliding away from me, reaching for the make-up remover she uses every time we touch. I watch her from the floor. I am high on the acetone. It is a comfort to me, as all routine sensations are. It is a religion of sorts. Karen is swiping at her naked belly, removing my greyness with cotton wool. She leaves snail-slick trails in her skin like the ghosts of old tears, already passed. She is telling me there will soon be a child. She is not using words. She is telling me this, along with other fears, in the particularly urgent way she cleans her belly, exposing the peachy skin beneath. She misses the spot on her cheek where I have chanced to kiss her with my grey statue lips. I wish I had the energy to reach out and bandage her in my arms, but even the smallest movement is problematic.

'Things will have to change round here,' she repeats. 'Everything's different since the baby.'

I lie very still on the carpet. My left sandal has come asunder, and the toe of it is winking at me from under the armchair. My naked foot makes me feel oddly unbalanced. I have always been a stickler for symmetry, as most statues are.

'You can't be selfish any more,' she continues. 'I need a husband I can lean on.'

'You can lean on me, Karen,' I say, ever so reassuringly, all the time wishing I had both sandals on. This makes my wife happy like a Christmas kid, for she reads the space behind my words and hears the very things she's always wanted to hear: 'I will be your proper husband now. I will get a real job, in a call centre if necessary. When the baby arrives I will also be a proper father and wear ordinary clothes such as jeans and sports shoes as I push my child around the shopping centre in a pram or buggy. I will no longer be an embarrassment to you in front of your friends.'

When I say, 'You can lean on me,' I am actually thinking about all the seagulls and individual passers-by who lean on me every day, pausing for one calm moment in the midst of all this hurtled living to catch their breath and settle. I remind myself that there is no man more solid, none more capable of being leant upon, than a statue. I am glad then for Karen and the baby just becoming inside her. There are luckier than they can possibly know or imagine, to be furnished with so much stillness.

My wife sees things from a different perspective. As one month trundles into the next and she stretches forwards and sideways to hold the baby in, Karen becomes more and more angry, occasionally throwing small items of furniture when she can no longer keep her loathing still.

'You're useless, so you are!' she shouts, as she flings the television remote at my forehead. 'Just sitting there, taking up space on the sofa.'

I do not move in time. Even the smallest movements require enormous amounts of planning now. The television remote clocks me squarely in the spot where my eyebrows meet. The next morning, I will have to apply an extra layer of pancake grey, to ensure that the bruise is not apparent.

'You can lean on me,' I remind Karen. 'I am not going anywhere.'

Dependability is a much underrated virtue. My wife, no doubt stirred to discontent by television chat shows and snippety friends and articles she's read on Facebook, does not think she wants a dependable husband. She thinks she wants someone faster, flightier, more active. Nothing I say will convince her otherwise.

In the final week before the baby arrives we barely talk.

'You will be there when it comes?' she asks over breakfast on Tuesday, the first words she's uttered in twenty-four hours. 'I'll phone when the labour starts.'

I smile at her across the table. It takes me almost an hour to eat a piece of toast these days. The coffee has long since gone frigid in my cup.

'Of course, I'll be there,' I reply. 'If the baby comes in the evening, or on a Sunday. You know I can't answer my phone when I'm statue-ing. I have to keep perfectly still.'

This is not what Karen wants to hear, so she doesn't listen. When I come home that evening, she is gone and the house is still as a glass tumbler. I stand in the corner for an hour before taking off my make-up. It is cold in the house, as if the outside has come indoors, and I can hear every individual thought writing itself inside my head:

I could get a personal driver to drive me to and from work so the bus is no longer an issue.

What about rolling out Beckett for the tourists this summer?

It's about time I took my sword to the cleaners. Or could I do it myself with polish?

And finally, the loudest of all thoughts: the cold thought that I am trying not to think about Karen and the baby, the way they grate against my stillness. No part of me is moving now, not even my heart. I might as well be a wall, I think, or a solid oak staircase. I am happy as I have never been in transit.

4.

Den and Estie Do Not Remember the Good Times

'There's something in my teeth,' says Estie.

'There's nothing in your teeth,' replies Den.

'How can you be sure, Denise? You're not inside my mouth.'

'Let me see then.'

Estie opens her mouth and leans across the kitchen table. Wide-eyed and jawing, she is like a baby bird stretched out for a worm. Den leans across the table to meet her mother, and for a moment, through the window, it must look as if they are going to kiss. They don't. There is a bitter-milk smell on Estie's breath. This comes from drinking too much tea and only brushing her teeth before bed. The taste of it gags at the back of Den's throat. She draws back sharply, pressing against the ribs of her chair.

'Look at my teeth,' commands Estie. Her mouth is still stretched open. Without lips, her words are soft and missing their angles. She lifts a stick finger, taps furiously at her front teeth and draws her lips back into a grotesque, donkey smile.

'OK, OK, stop that. I'll look at your teeth.'

Den lifts the mobile phone from her cardigan pocket and switches the screen light on. She takes a quick glance inside her mother's mouth. The inside of Estie's mouth is the colour of stored meat. Her tongue is furred white and lardy yellow in dots along the spine. Den can see the wired lines where her dentures are fixed to the front of her gums. She counts the gunmetal dips of one, two, three fillings crowning her backmost molars. There are bread-paste triangles between Estie's front teeth. They have been there since breakfast. They could be easily hoaked out with the edge of a thumbnail, but Estie does not like to have her teeth touched. She hasn't been to the dentist in years.

Den cannot see anything particularly sinister in her mother's mouth.

'There's nothing in your teeth, Mum,' she says. 'It was probably just a bit of toast that's shifted now.'

Estie clamps her mouth shut. She stands up, leaning her full weight against the table.

'You only looked, Denise,' she howls. 'You never listened.'

'You can't hear teeth, Mum,' Den replies, though once, late at night on local radio, she'd heard about a woman whose metal fillings could pick up the signals from taxi cabs and police-car radios. She is sure this is not happening to her mother. It is likely that the story was part of a radio play and not intended to be taken seriously.

'You're not listening hard enough, Denise. You've never been good at listening.'

'I'm listening to you now, Mum. I don't listen to anyone else these days.'

'If you were listening properly, you'd be hearing the thing in my teeth.'

Den humours her mother. She turns her head to face the kitchen door so her right ear is inclined towards Estie's open mouth. She braces herself against the table edge, ready to duck back at the first sharp movement. These days there is every possibility that she may be bitten. She listens with her eyes closed, as if she is listening very intently or perhaps praying.

She hears the foggy purr of her mother's breath, the fridge mumbling in the corner, the rain and possibly the wind, but not the slightest hint of teeth.

'What am I listening for?' she asks. 'What is it you think's in your teeth?'

'God,' says Estie.

Den is relieved to hear this. God, she can manage. Yesterday it was Samuel talking out of her mother's teeth. Samuel is Den's father; or rather, was Den's father. Samuel is dead now and this, for some reason, is a concept more difficult to explain to Estie than the possibility of a live man in her mouth, speaking.

'God, indeed,' Den repeats patiently. 'And what is God saying inside your mouth?'

'Oh, this and that, and some singing. He says you're an awful good wee girl not to be leaving your mammy by herself.'

'Really? Well, it sounds like God's the most sensible thing to come out of your mouth this week, Mum.'

Den smiles, and tries to laugh. It sticks in her.

Estie doesn't laugh. Humour with words is beyond her. She only laughs at people falling over now and things being dropped and other unplanned acts of clumsiness. In the past, she had a wit as sharp as a piece of paper folded and folded again. Everything about her is blunt now, except the hitting.

Den takes her mother's face in both hands and presses gently so that the old lady's lips purse open like a clamshell. She peers into the black space of her mouth and says, in a pedantic, childly voice, 'It's so good to finally meet you, God. Will you be sticking around for lunch?' She makes herself feel clever inside when she says this. These funny moments would be more enjoyable if she had a sane person to catch by the eye and wink, but Den must still grab them when she can. Sometimes she imagines recounting them as humorous anecdotes to friends or work colleagues – a husband, ideally. This never happens. There is only Estie now and occasionally the social worker. The social worker has approximately twelve minutes per visit. She measures out the minutes on her phone and when she is done an alarm goes off like baby birds cheeping. The social worker has too little time to waste any on hearing funny things which have happened during the previous week.

For a moment, Den holds her mother's face between her hands. She sees herself reflected in the black parts of Estie's eyes and wonders who the old lady is seeing.

Estie lifts her arms from her lap. She places her hands on top of Den's hands, so they are a vice holding her own jaw together. There is a game which children play that is like this, with hands on top of other hands and rhyming. Estie is not playing this game, though sometimes she is more of a child than a full-grown adult. She digs her fingernails into the flesh of Den's wrists, leaves ten pink crescents in her skin, like the marks from an ill-fitting bracelet.

'Don't laugh at me,' she hisses. She peels Den's hands away from her face. 'Don't you dare laugh at me!'

She could be talking to Den. She could be talking to God. She could possibly be addressing both of them and also the condiment bottles soldiering themselves against the wall. There is always the ghost of a conversation, like a one-way street, running out of Estie. People are inside her head, or she is inside her own head, or there is nothing inside her head but the echo of a conversation from yesterday or the day before. No matter how many books Den reads on the subject, she can never be quite sure what her mother is hearing in the silence. Then, Estie is crying and thumping at her own face with the fist of her curled right hand. She reaches inside her mouth and runs her fingernails down her tongue, like a small child, trying to scrape the bad taste out.

'There is something in my teeth!' she screams.

Den and Estie have been here five times already this week. This is the first time with God. Den has learnt what to do next. Lately, Den has been learning more quickly. She rarely resorts to the on-call doctor now.

'Take your teeth out, Mum,' she says quite calmly. 'It's time for bed.'

She pulls the curtains across the kitchen window to disguise the morning. The sun is too strong for the thin, floral fabric. It makes the curtains glow. It is unlikely that Estie will notice this and if she does Den will make up some lie about full moons or streetlamps. Den is getting better and better at telling lies. She fills a clean glass of water from the tap and sets it in front of her mother. She is smiling, smiling, smiling as if she is the parent and Estie is the child and this is something they do every night before bed.

'Is it bedtime?' Estie asks. Den is relieved to see that the distraction has taken.

'Yes, Mum, it's time for bed. Do you want a hot-water bottle?'

The old lady nods knowingly and removes her dentures. A string of saliva comes with them and, for a moment, Estie is joined to her teeth by a thin yard of spider thread. She stares at the dentures briefly, as if trying to see God hiding between the cracks in her teeth, then she drops them into the water. The teeth drown. God falls silent. Things return to normal, or what they have lately come to mistake for normal.

Den makes a cup of tea. Every time she feels like crying she puts the kettle on instead; so many cups of tea. The paint is beginning to peel off where the kettle steam condenses beneath the kitchen units. She boils the kettle fifteen times a day at least. Den likes to hold a tea mug until it goes cold. The burn of it in her palms reminds her that there are other ways to feel pain. She rarely bothers drinking the tea.

Sometime later it is lunch. Estie has forgotten about God and put her teeth back in. She has done television and climbing the stairs and is caught in a new loop now. Her mind is taking her out for the night, for dinner or perhaps dancing. Though it's over a month since she last left the house, she is obsessing over the details of her outfit. She is worrying about how she will appear in the eyes of other women. Insecurity is a new language for Estie, but Den suspects there has always been this third eye inside her mother, quietly judging.

'Do you think I can get away with this dress?' Estie asks. 'Pink hasn't always been the easiest colour for me.' She is wearing a pair of tracksuit bottoms today and a cardigan layered over a pullover.

'Too much lipstick?'

'Hair up or hair down?'

Estie reaches over her shoulder to the place where her hair once hung and scoops the air into an imaginary ponytail. She holds the absence of hair one-handed at the base of her skull as if it were the first taut throb of a headache, or a hat twitching in the wind.

'What do you think, Denise? Hair up or hair down?'

Den turns from the tinned soup gargling on the stove. They will have this soup for lunch with bread and then again, with boiled potatoes, for tea. She sees her mother framed in the kitchen doorway, moving her head stiffly from left to right, all chin and sucked-in cheekbones, like a young girl posturing in the bathroom mirror. In the soft margarine light, the veins on Estie's neck are pale grey, the colour of common pigeons, and just about visible beneath her skin.

Den can still see the place where her mother was beautiful as a younger woman. It is round her eyes and in the slight pinch of her upper lip.

'Hair down, Mum,' she says, dragging a spoon through the soup loosely, in the shape of a figure eight. The clink of it tinning against the saucepan's sides is a way of letting the tightness out. Den wishes to add, 'You don't have enough hair for a ponytail any more, Mum,' but Estie is no longer listening. She has distracted herself with the mother-of-pearl buttons on her blouse and is humming softly as she fuddles the little disks in and out of their sockets. This sometimes happens. The old lady is quick to fixate upon beads and zippers, her eyes constantly going for a good place to settle. More often, however, she catches on her own anxiety. She will ask a question and hover round the edge of it, like a nervous fruit fly, repeating it for hours or even days.

Den has taught herself how to answer without listening. This is the best way to keep from hitting Estie or leaving her alone in a locked room.

'Soup OK for lunch, Mum?' she asks.

'Soup,' repeats Estie, 'soup, soup, soup.' She rolls the word round her mouth as if looking for an entry point. She cannot find it. 'Shall I wear the pearls tonight?'

It is February. The kitchen lights are already on though it's barely turned afternoon. Den is careful to switch the lights off when she leaves a room. Estie does not remember that they must save money now. She trails through the house like a restless child, leaving the television on, the fridge door open and the lights loud in every room.

'Your house is like the Blackpool Illuminations these days,' says Mr McNally across the road. 'Youse must have the money to burn.'

Money to burn is the last thing Den has. She does not say this to Mr McNally, or any of the people who knew her parents when they had the shop and the holiday house in Portstewart. Neither does she tell the social worker, when she pops in to check up on Esti (friendly like, but still writing everything in her notepad).

'Remember, Mum,' Den says firmly, 'we sold the pearls after Daddy died? To pay for the funeral.'

Estie lifts a hand to her neck, sketches the circle of her collar as if the pearls are still there rising and rolling against her throat. The nails on her fingers are long and dirty yellow like the skeleton teeth of animals in a museum. Den makes a note to clip them before bed. While she's at it, she will also try to do the old lady's toenails. This may be more than she can manage alone. Lately, Estie has taken to screaming and slicing out. There is a blue-black circle on the underside of Den's wrist, like the almost-washed-off stamp from a nightclub door. Her mother left this on her with the remote. At the time, she'd been trying to watch her cooking show and the sound from the television had been too loud or possibly, too low. Den cannot remember which. Details do not matter any more, nor even stick, though she sometimes recalls tiny asides like stills from the cine film which is their old life: the time her mother did her tea with milk and golden syrup to cut the caffeine's bite, the cotton hankies folded and tucked inside her cardigan cuff, the way she once sang hymns at the kitchen sink, her voice bouncing off the double-glazing so she sounded like a chorus of herself.

The bruise on Den's wrist is almost gone now and easy to cover with a sweater sleeve.

'Daddy is dead?' Estie says for the first time today. Her voice climbs a hill so it is a question she is making rather than a statement. After all these years it is hard to believe she has forgotten and, from time to time, Den still wonders if all this, even the hitting, is some kind of elaborate joke. Her mother looks so good, so very good for a woman of eighty, not failed at all.

'You'd never know to look at her would you?' Mr McNally says, when he comes across Estie and Den sitting together on the bus. He whispers this as if the old lady is foreign or hard of hearing and only Den will catch the meaning behind his mouth. Den wants to tell him that it doesn't matter any more, that she often loses the run of herself and shouts at her mother, 'You're doting, Mum! You've got dementia!' Rarely do the words even land in the right place. These days, Estie cries when she should be laughing and sometimes wakes the night house up hooting like a lunatic.

'At least Mum still has her health,' she replies. This is a strange and slanted thing to say, given the fact that Estie is ill in the head. Forgetting yourself is worse to live with than arthritis, or losing the sight in both eyes, or even cancer.

'You're right there, Denise. At least she has her good health,' Mr McNally repeats, smiling all over his face. He has the look of a wedding priest about him, far too anxious to please. Every time she sees him on the bus, Den tries to get away, but there are only so many places you can go in a moving vehicle and Estie drags on her like an anchor.

The smaller her mother shrinks the heavier she seems to feel. Once solid, Estie is now a bird of a woman. She is bent along the middle as if caught in a long study of her own slippered toes. Yet the weight of her wakes Den up in the middle of the night. She worries constantly. The feel of it is a pain in her ribcage, as if worry is made of sand and the sand has gathered inside her and cannot be shifted while lying down. She lies awake for hours turning the pillow over for a cold spot, wondering how she has arrived back here in her childhood bedroom with the same shelves and cloud-print curtains.

Every so often Den wishes Estie were dead. She only entertains these thoughts in bed, picturing the funeral, the grave and the kind things people will say in cards such as, 'She was so proud of you, Denise,' and, 'You are a real credit to her.' In bed, she can pretend these thoughts are dreams and that they have slipped out of her accidentally, without intent.

In the morning her mother is usually calmer. She lifts her arms for a hug and Den feels the guilt lumping between them like a thick sweater. It is hard to hold onto Estie, knowing all the things she has just allowed herself to think. When she has enough energy, Den feels sorry for both of them equally. On difficult days she prioritises herself. She tells herself there would have been a husband if it weren't for Estie. Of course this isn't true, but it helps to have something solid to hook her disappointment on.

'Yes, Mum,' she says, today, as she's said every day for the last month, 'your daddy is dead, and my daddy is dead, and there's only the two of us left to look after each other now.'

Estie sits down at the kitchen table and draws her cardigan around her ribs, tucking one wing over the other. She wears her clothes like bandages, layering shirts and sweaters, blouses and cardigans one on top of the other until she is four inches thicker all the way round. 'Self-protection', the social worker calls it, and says it's not uncommon in older people. Den worries about her mother overheating. Dehydration is the worst thing that can happen to a person with dementia – dehydration and falling over.

Estie cries. She goes fishing up her sleeve for a clean cotton hankie and finds, instead, a wad of yesterday's Kleenex. Austerity has brought the age of clean cotton hankies to an end. Estie cries every time she hears that her father is dead. Watching her is like watching Den's DVD of *Romeo and Juliet*, which is snagged during the chapel scene. Her Leonardo DiCaprio is stuck in a loop, finding Claire Danes dead amongst the candles over and over again, as if he hasn't seen any of this coming and won't remember it thirty seconds later.

Den has grown accustomed to the tears. Each time she breaks the bad news to her mother she tries to be touching her: a hand on her arm, an arm around her shoulder, a forehead leaning against her mother's forehead as if they are lovers comforting each other. She has read in a magazine that old people, particularly those with dementia, find touch reassuring.

She tells her grandfather's passing like it is not twenty-five years since he died but just this morning, and he is still upstairs in the spare room waiting quietly for the undertaker to arrive.

'He'd a good, long life, Mum,' she says, 'and such a blessing to go in his sleep. Sure, he wouldn't even have known he was dying.'

She hopes this will be a comfort to Estie, even though it is a lie. Her grandfather died slowly with the cancer, the side of his face mottling and then peeling away like rotten meat. Her father died in a car crash off the Dunsilly roundabout: screech, crunch, shatter and dead before the ambulance arrived. Estie is too far gone to distinguish between these close deaths and the distant ones on the television news. Yet she still cries.

Estie is selfish when she is sad. She does not think for a moment that Den might be entitled to a slice of this grief. Everything is only happening to her and always in the moment.

'Did you know my daddy?' she asks Den. She could just as easily be talking to the postman or the lady who used to clean the shop. 'He was a real gentleman,' she continues, 'the last of a dying breed.'

'He was indeed, Mum,' replies Den. She is never quite sure if her mother is talking about her father, or her grandfather, or some muddled splice of both men, wearing a bowler hat.

There is no comfort for Den in this ritual. The soft words

and the laying on of hands are another thing she has to do now, every day, like the measuring out of tablets and the hair brushing and the rigmarole with the living-room curtains, which have taken over from the backyard sparrows as Estie's latest fixation. She feels as if there is a hole at the bottom of her throat and all the eagerness is leaving her in drips. She does not allow herself to cry. Once she starts she will never stop, and what use would she be to Estie then? There is no one to take over from her, even for a weekend.

In the past, when Estie was simply old and not quite so forgotten, Den muddled through with lists and a kind of stoic bluster. She still tries, but the effort required is a ragged sort of burden to carry alone, like going upstairs with a sharp-angled parcel.

'Shall we get you nice and clean before bed, Mum? Open wide for a big bite of cornflakes. Let's pop you into some fresh pants,' Den repeats these phrases, once, twice, three times a day. This easy, breezy voice does not sound like herself speaking, but it helps Den hold the distance between now and how they once were in each other's company.

She has not been surprised by the indignity of it all, the brute moments in the bathroom, covering her own mother's nakedness with a towel. Den has read books from the library and talked, at length, with the social worker. She is prepared for everything, even the piss and shit. When the time comes, she will approach her mother as a stranger. Faced with soiled sheets and incontinence pads, she will call the old lady Estie, not Mum or Mother. This will be easier for both of them, like a kind of acting. Den is willing and almost ready to shoulder her mother through the next decline.

But the sadness has come out of nowhere. Den has not anticipated it. Neither did it feature in any of the library books.

She does not know whether to ignore Estie when she cries, or pull up a chair and join in. Her mother has, until now, been the sunniest of women, if somewhat aloof. There are concertina lines around her eyes and mouth, the fossilised remains of eighty years' hard smiling. Den has no such lines on her face.

'You're lucky, Denise,' the social worker has often told her. 'Your mum's not violent or distressed. It's harder on you than her. Estie's happy as Larry in her own wee world.'

It is clear to Den that her mother is no longer as happy as Larry or as happy as the day is long or even a pig in mud. Her mother is almost always crying or on the verge. She is thinking about calling the social worker up and saying, 'Mum's been crying for a solid month,' but she holds off. She is afraid that the social worker will assume it is her fault. This might affect their benefits. The benefits are the only thing keeping them in tinned soup and Rich Teas.

At the table, Estie is rocking backwards and forwards on a stackable stool, the front legs lifting and lowering as her movements become increasingly violent. 'The pearls are gone. Daddy is gone,' she repeats, 'Daddy is gone. The pearls are gone.' It is impossible to tell which loss she is feeling most keenly today.

Den puts a hand on her shoulder, tries to stop the rocking. She can feel the sobs gathering speed inside her mother, progressing through her body like the last tight cramps of childbirth.

Once again she considers phoning her mother's sister in Larne, explaining everything from the beginning. She could tell her aunt that money is so tight they are squeezing six pots out of every tea bag, that they live on value-pack biscuits and do their underwear in the bath for fear of wasting electricity on the washing machine. She could make it sound like necessity has forced her to ask for help, and Aunty Kathleen will make sympathetic noises and say, 'It's not your fault Love. You're doing your best,' and, 'Maybe it's time to think about a home.' She might even offer to pop a cheque in the post.

Den could do this and never get the good of the confession for she will still feel guilty every time she looks at Estie. The guilt is not something she can explain with words or even write down.

It is something to do with an afternoon from ever so long ago which comes back to Den in fragments, first thing in the morning and on the toilet with the bathroom door locked, which is her only way of guaranteeing three minutes' peace. Back then, she'd still had a mother and a father and they'd been on their holidays in England, by the coast. It had definitely been a sunny day, because Den remembers the particular blue of sky against sea, warm for England. They'd parked the car by the pier, walked along the edge of the beach and come across a whole troupe of old folks. They were lined along the sand in deck chairs with travel rugs binding their legs into mermaid tails.

Even as a child, Den had known these were not people like her parents. These were very old people, another species entirely, gone in the head and chittering to themselves as ancient machines chitter in factories. She'd been a little afraid of them and reached for her father's hand, though she was too old, by this stage, for hand-holding. As they'd walked past, she noticed that the old people were eating ice creams – the whippy sort, in cones – and most of it was drooling down their chins and over their fingers like the white part of seagull shit. There was something of the animal about the way they ate. She had not wanted to look at them for too long and yet found herself staring.

Once they'd gained enough distance to go unheard, her father turned to her mother and said, 'Dear love them, Estie, with their ice creams.' He'd smiled then at his girls, a smile like the memory of a good meal. 'Isn't it grand that the home's brought them on a wee run to the seaside?'

Den's mother had not thought it was grand at all. She'd stopped on the edge of the beach and snapped at her husband like a pair of kitchen scissors. 'If that was me, Samuel, slabbering all over my own jumper, I wouldn't want to be paraded down the prom for the world to see. The place for people like that's at home with their families. There's no one but your own kin should see you in that state.' Afterwards she'd walked on ahead of them and there were curls in the sand from where her feet had been angry and turned.

Den has always remembered the curls in the sand and the cut of her mother's legs striding away from them, across the beach, towards the car like two cold pillars rising from her summer sandals. This is what her guilt looks like every time she lifts the telephone and imagines the various aunts and social workers and nursing homes attached to it by strong, electric wires. This is what her guilt looks like. The guilt also tastes like sand in her mouth when she wishes for another person to look upon her mother slobbering or naked on the bathroom floor. What the guilt sounds like is God in her mouth, always howling. Den tries sometimes with her fingers, but she cannot remove her teeth or make it stop.

5.

In Feet and Gradual Inches

I was under the bed when Emily died.

I'd been under the bed all day Wednesday and most of Tuesday, watching their feet approach and recede like soft brown boats scouting for a safe place to berth. Hands could fold and faces lie, but anchored to the spare-room carpet, their feet betrayed a holy horror of the bed and the sheets and my sister who was not quite there any more. I watched their feet through a gap in the valance: my father's boots with muddied toes, the doctor's determined heels and my mother's brogues, laces unravelling like her own washday hair, in strands and greasy slips.

When they came close, to kiss Emily, to fuss the pillows or take her tumbling pulse, I made myself a Jesus cross just like on a stained glass window: straight legs, spread arms and sad head, hanging. I reached far out into the room and grazed my fingers against their shoes, up and softly down. Their feet spoke to me, sweating through rubber soles and leather uppers to ask if the real adults would be arriving soon and when they might be permitted to leave. They did not feel my fingers grabbing at their heels, only the power as it left them.

Even the doctor did not notice me, though he was paid to catch the hair's-breadth detail between one breath and the next.

You'd think, I thought, and could not believe my own selfishness, *they'd miss me, even now, with my sister almost gone and fading.*

Still, they did not notice me present beneath her bed nor absent from the places where I could usually be found: upside down on the good-room sofa, at the table with cornflakes, on the swing set dangling over the front lawn like a bad-luck charm.

One down, I thought, and could not believe my own cool head, *one perfectly good child left to have and to hold against the coming winter. Surely, there should be more of me when Emily goes.*

But they saw things differently, my mother and father. One down and their world had fallen into itself: ceiling, walls and every ordinary brick undoing until there was nothing left to lend perspective, nothing to run parallel with their grief.

My sister had been the only thing in our house for days. You could feel the awful thickness of her every time you entered a room. Of course there were other fixtures and fittings we'd also grown accustomed to: doors, window frames, a larder stocked with last year's jam, a short-wave radio resting on the shelf above the fridge. Sometimes it spoke and sometimes it fell silent. The radio reminded us, every hour on the hour, that other people in other places were also anxious, suffering from civil war, tax evasion and the very real possibility of an AIDS epidemic. It was impossible to believe in these people or their far away problems. My sister had been the only thing in the world for days now.

Beneath the bed, with all of Emily hanging heavily above me, I was sure that satellites and other circling parties could see her from space, the weight of my sister broadcasting its presence to the heavens with an authority rivalling the Great Wall or those deeper, wider oceans.

From beneath the bed, Emily was just a dent in the mattress.

I pressed my nose against the place where her head should have been and measured myself: four feet and a handful of greedy inches. We were small for our age, my sister and I, no bigger than a pair of upright golf bags. Mother was tall, and father taller. We often wondered where we'd come from, only lately understanding that twins were separate people and not a single person divided neatly in two. Everything about us matched – eyes, arms, yellow-ish hair – everything except our feet, which differed by one size and had always been the objects of prayer and much earnest concern. We could not bear to be different in anything, even the inconsequentials. Emily prayed for less and I prayed for more. Our feet remained odd and ill-inclined to change.

In the end, Emily took the matter into her own hands.

On Wednesday morning, whilst my father fed the cows and my mother fixed breakfast in the kitchen below, my sister removed her pyjama bottoms, ran the bath and stood ankle deep in boiling water. She'd heard on a television advertisement that hot water shrank things and assumed that bone and sweating flesh were subject to the same rules as a dry-clean sweater. The scream of her, running down the pipes and through the air-conditioning vents, was thin as hoar frost. It stripped the bathroom clean of mildew for a fortnight after. By the time my mother had untangled herself from the kitchen sink and leapt the stairs in hungry strides, Emily was underwater, floating: a raw-meat mess of herself, still wearing pants and the buttoned-up top of her Christmas pyjamas.

She was pink when they hauled her out, then red and finally a putrid yellow, though the heat had not affected her eyes, which remained blue, and jittered back and forth in their sockets like a pair of pinball marbles. My mother's arms blushed a similar shade of sausage, to the elbow, where the water caught her, once again dragging my sister to the surface of things. My mother refused to wear bandages and swore she could not feel the pain. I knew she was lying, for her lips curled like a backyard dog's each time she touched a spoon or door handle.

'What were you thinking, Emily?' asked my father, in the dark, with his big shoes angled like a set of empty brackets. He did not know that I was beneath the bed, listening. Neither did he expect an answer.

My sister could not speak. Her whole face was the colour of tongue, and the thought of words had already left her. I spoke for her, pushing my mouth deep into the mattress where her head was heaviest so she heard these last true things filtered through cloth and springs, summer blankets and kindly feathers.

'We are four feet and a handful of inches, yellow hair and blue eyes, two legs, two arms, two hands and ears, a single mouth and one nose, a set of breasts just beginning to surface and a pair of feet, shoe size three.' (I did not start into the internal organs or think it kind to mention that the hot, hot water had pickled Emily, bloating her like a beached corpse. We were stranger in our own skins than we'd ever been.)

I could not see her mouth, but I felt her smile and knew the pain of this, her burnt lips peeling backwards like cooked ham slices. Beneath the bed my throat caught on itself and settled. Emily left, smiling. In her very last moment, my sister was punched beef and two rows of pearly headstones. God himself, staring into that face, could not have split the difference between a grin and a grimace, but I knew. I knew and I did not tell.

I was under the bed when Emily died. The room did not move. Nothing entered. Nothing left, but my father leant suddenly forward and back as if swayed by some ungodly current. My mother made the noise of a trapped cough and hunkered down on the bedroom carpet; a small child preparing to leap or topple. The arm closest to me was raw-meat red as it clasped her knees. Her skirt was caught up in a most undignified manner. She had the look of a much older woman. I reached through the valance and touched the tip of my mother's shoe, just once where the leather had scuffed away. It was hotter than a shoe should ever be.

'She's gone,' said my father. Beneath Emily's bed the dent in the mattress defied him. It remained deep and deft, weight spread equally across four feet and a handful of heavy inches.

'It's empty in here without her,' he said. My mother nodded assent with her whole body. Heel to toe. Toe to heel. Keening softly as she rocked.

The house was emptier without my sister. Her absence grew to fill the rooms and cupboards, sliding down the back of the dishwasher till there was not so much as a square inch left to hold me. I did not move. I did not move a single shivering muscle. I thought it best not to breathe for fear that in shifting a fingernail's sleight to left or right, I might sacrifice my own corner.

I was no stranger to emptiness, even then. Our parents, expecting one and receiving two, had raised us thin and quick on home-grown vegetables and the last deft licks of an army pension. I was no stranger to emptiness and all its bastard sons. I had often known the dry end of a milk bottle, also car parks, biscuit tins and next-door-but-one with its boarded up windows. The removal of a tooth and the salt-gum hole which mourned its passing. Great Aunt Irene, who howled for hours at the empty room where her cats had once lived. Ten years' worth of Easter tombs, each complete with a rolling rock and an angel host. Certain sections of the Central Library.

Emptiness, I knew without saying, was just another word for anticipation; the dry pause before filling; the memory of a good, true thing sucked and sucked again like a boiled sweet dissolving on the tongue.

Emily left a different kind of emptiness behind. It was a cloud and then the roof came down so there was no room for anything, even God, who, I'd been led to believe, was more than capable of squeezing through the thin places.

Everyone arriving at our house said, 'It's empty in here without Emily,' or, 'You'll feel the house empty now she's gone,' or words to this effect, with similar intonation. Their voices were spades and spoons, dig, dig, digging a wide trench between my parents' emptiness and their own front doors, which still said, 'Welcome', and 'Home Sweet Home', in the sort of dirt-proof lettering most people chose to believe in. They did not stay long in our house. The emptiness forced them out the door and down the path, to the front gate and the gravelling roads beyond where there was finally air enough to breathe.

I was under the bed when the doctor came, also my aunts on both sides, the next-door neighbours and various ladies who brought casseroles and Bible prayers, neither of which my mother had stomach for. She was too polite to spit in their presence. She took their concern graciously, shelving it, like last year's jam, at the back of the larder. No one asked after me. No one noticed my absence, even the best of all aunts and her Southern boyfriend.

Once, the Southern boyfriend said, 'There's something missing here. Some small detail.' He looked round and round Emily's room, his blue eyes beaming in wide, concentric circles.

Beneath the bed I clamped a hand over my mouth and said, oh so very quietly through my fingers, 'It's me, it's me you're looking for.' My heart was in my throat and my throat was in my mouth. My mouth was caught like corn grass in my teeth and could not see a way through.

'It's the cat you're missing,' said my father. 'The cat went under the bin lorry last Tuesday, chasing a mouse or a bird or something, and that was the end of the cat.'

'Splat,' said my father and made a hand-slam motion with both palms open.

'I suspect you're right, sir,' said the Southern boyfriend. He folded his hands, one over the other like a church amen, and that was the end of that.

I was still under the bed when the Measuring Man arrived. He stood next to my father and asked 'How tall was your daughter?' His voice was nicely, nicely, fog and tissue paper. His shoes, the most certain things I'd ever seen. Even then I might have said, 'I'm under here. I'm your answer. Measure me,' but I did not dare speak nor show myself in the presence of those shoes.

My father said, 'My daughter was this big,' with his arms like an open mouth and ordered two boxes: one for my sister and one to fill the space she'd left behind.

The first box sank, dragging Emily with it.

The second box stood like a wayside pulpit in the corner of my sister's room. The colour of it was sand: ordinary beach sand, not the holiday kind. Three brass hinges ribbed it shut on the left side, a keyhole and a clever little key on the right. My father balanced a bedside lamp on top of the box – pink with a corrugated frill for a shade – and ran an extension cord all the way under the bedroom rug to the plug socket beside Emily's bed. He kept the light switched on: a pillar of fire by night, by day, a birthday candle, mumbling in the sun. 'So we can always see it,' he said, and I remembered from school the Egyptians and their hulking, pointed pyramids, their reluctance to let things slip quietly into the past. I felt ashamed for my father and also afraid. He had not slept for days and only spoke when the box was listening.

The box was the exact head-to-heel size of Emily, my father's brave attempt at filling all those feet and empty inches she'd left behind. From beneath the bed, without moving, I could see the last squat third of it. It did not have a face or feet. It could not sing or recite, without looking, every line of the 23rd Psalm. It did not smell faintly of Vosene shampoo. It had never once fallen asleep next to me, head to toe, fitting like a pair of pickled herrings. Planted in the corner of the room, the carpet had puckered slightly around each edge, as if frowning beneath its weight. It towered over the bookcase, terrified the sock drawer and blocked all but the most determined draughts of sunlight. These, and other observations, were more than enough to convince me that a box was no good excuse for a sister.

'No difference,' announced my father, though no one had asked. 'No difference at all between Emily and the box. I measured. They're exactly the same. Don't try telling me the house is empty without her. It's just as full as it's ever been.'

My mother agreed. My mother agreed with almost everything my father ever said. Sometimes she agreed with things my father had not even said yet. My mother was a very agreeable kind of woman. However, on this particular occasion she could not stand in agreement. She found herself sitting heavily on the bedroom carpet, drawn to the floor suddenly. Clump. Thud. My mother made the sound of meat falling. Later, she would wonder why my father's words had dragged on her like hammers and gusting wind, and realise that the box was the largest thing he'd ever asked her to agree upon. In the future she would sit down every time he asked her a question, preparing as best she could for larger boxes, for houses, hills and perhaps one day, a medium-sized mountain.

Every day after Emily, and especially before breakfast, my mother had the look of a much older woman. She anointed the box, morning and evening, going at it furiously with an old tea towel and the same furniture polish she used on the dining-room table. It was not quite my sister but it gave her something to do with her hands when the twitching took hold.

The room, without my sister, began to smell like church and synthetic flowers. It was impossible to tell if the box was to blame, or whether it was subject to the same sad aroma as the rest of us.

My father poked his head into Emily's room each time he passed the open door. He nodded at the box and smiled. Occasionally he took a measuring tape to it, checking earnestly, and with clipped precision, that the room was just as full as it had ever been. My father smiled all the time, even in the dark when the lamps weren't looking, ear-to-ear like a sliced melon. The smile sewed him together. Without it he was afraid his face might fall off.

At night while my father told himself he was sleeping and my mother lay straight beside him, picking individual threads from the sleeve of her nightdress, I crept out from beneath my sister's bed and placed small items inside the box, one item per night for three straight weeks. A jar of peanut butter, unopened. A scrubbing brush. A twenty-pence piece. A clean flannel and a desert fork. Two sports socks, balled in a fist. Scissors and a pair of my father's reading glasses. A *National Geographic*, hoping, as I placed it amidst the mumbling detritus of our old lives, for a dose of global perspective.

I dared my parents good, but they did not notice the money or the scissors. Or the glasses –though, in his defence, my father had not read a book in years.

I was under the bed when they noticed the peanut butter was missing. I expect they were making sandwiches. It had been weeks since they'd made a meal requiring anything more taxing than a tin opener.

'Something's missing,' said my mother, her voice itching through the air-conditioning vents, along the corridor from the kitchen to my sister's bedroom, 'I could have sworn we had a jar of peanut butter in the larder.'

'You're imagining it,' answered my father. 'The house is just as full as it's ever been.'

There were charts he could have shown my mother had she bothered to ask: an almost full notebook, with each day's measurements carefully noted in royal-blue biro. Four feet three inches, never deviating more than an eyelash to left or right of the measuring tape. My mother did not ask for proof. In the grander scheme of things, peanut butter seemed a small and infinitely manageable concession. She sat herself down on a foldable chair and wholeheartedly agreed.

Under the bed I felt like a lost coastline.

That night, while my father thought about all the times he had, in the past, slept deeply and thickly through storms and winter winds, and my mother lay straight beside him plucking individual hairs from the crown of her head like an early bird worming, I crept out from beneath my sister's bed and went rummaging through her wardrobe for a pair of school shoes, one size too big but wearable with thicker socks. Removing the scrubbing brush, the twenty-pence piece, the scissors and reading glasses, the unopened jar of peanut butter and the *National Geographic*, I climbed inside the box and closed the door behind me.

My father was right. It was exactly the size of my sister inside.

It was empty in the box without her, and difficult to breathe. I closed my eyes, though this was entirely unnecessary on account of the darkness, and I wondered, in the morning, if my father would wake uneasy, if my mother would find the house emptier without me.

6.

We've Got Each Other
and That's a Lot

Dad has his Bon Jovi tape on again. He likes a bit of Jon Bon and the boys while we're waiting for my brother. The music makes him feel like a getaway driver from a film. This is a hard feeling to fake when you drive a Citroen Saxo (two doors, not four). For a while there, he even wore a bandana and a jeans jacket with the sleeves ripped off. There were thin, white threads like feathers sprouting from his shoulders, as if the stuffing was coming out of him, or his wings had fallen off.

'What in God's name are you wearing, Samuel?' said Mammy, the first time she saw him in his bandit gear. 'You look like a woman in that get up.'

She said the word 'woman' to sound like 'wee man', which is the way they say it round here.

After this, Dad quit wearing his jeans jacket. 'Too conspicuous if the cops catch us,' he said. He said this as if he'd considered all the angles and arrived at the decision by himself. My dad couldn't choose left over right without consulting Mammy first.

Still, I could tell it was a relief for him to get a jumper back on. He's never done well with the cold. It brings him out in red pimples like he's taking an allergic reaction to himself.

It's always cold 'round here, even in the summer. When we have enough money, or my brother gets too old to sell, we're for moving to Australia.

'They're crying out for skilled workers over there,' says my dad, 'and it's always roasting. Most folks have a swimming pool in their back garden.'

I sometimes wonder which of his skills Dad thinks is the best: gutting chickens, waiting in parked cars or thieving money off young married couples. I know better than to ask.

'Them Australians will be lucky to have us,' I say. Dad reaches over the driver's seat to give me a backwards high five.

He hasn't noticed yet that the fabric on the corners of the Saxo's front seats has been gnawed away to reveal the yellow padding beneath. I have done this with my teeth while we are waiting. There is nothing to do in a parked car and Mammy will not allow me to sleep.

'You've to be on your toes, Paddy,' she says, 'primed and ready for action.' By this she means that I'm the one who's to fold the front seat forward and let my brother in the back when he comes running. I am what you might call an integral part of the whole operation. I'd feel a lot more important though, if I had a gun or some sort of disguise.

We spend a lot of time waiting in the car with the heaters off. It is colder behind the glass than outside. I can see my breath curling over my parents' heads in whispers. My mammy used to laugh at this and say, 'Look at the cut of us, like fire-breathing dragons.' She used to tell jokes to pass the time. 'Knock, knock.' 'Doctor, doctor.' 'Did you hear the one about the blind priest?' Now she doesn't say anything any more. We sit in the dark and count the money up in our heads. This is a bit like praying when you don't use words.

- Five grand off the Montgomerys in Portstewart.

- Another five from the folks in the big bungalow outside Lisnaskea.

- Six grand in Markethill last December.

- Eight thousand euro from the Gormans in Portlaoise (the only time we've ventured into the Free State).

- Plus ten thousand or so in jewellery and small, untraceable electronic items which my mammy is selling on eBay. She is using a false name of course, lifted from a girl in Larne who used to do her hair.

Mammy's careful to keep a fair amount of distance between one family and the next. There's always the fear that a couple might have told someone about us, especially in the country, where there is little else to be talking about. We go backwards and forwards across the province, putting wee adverts in the local papers: 'Struggling to start a family?' 'Frustrated by long waiting lists for adoption?'

Mammy has a mobile just for the adverts. When it goes off, the ringtone is the theme tune from *The Littlest Hobo,* which is a programme about a travelling dog she used to watch when she was a wee girl. The song always makes her smile, even when she's just been shouting at my dad. She knows to answer the phone in her sad voice because the calls are always about my brother.

'Yes,' Mammy says. She can sound like she's near crying on the telephone. 'I'm at my wits' end. I can't give the child what he needs. I'm heart feared his da's going to come home and lay into him again.'

She always gives them a price straight off, something around the twenty grand mark. This is what they decided my brother was worth. He's not a baby any more. We could ask more for a baby. They're better value for money because you get longer with them. We don't have a baby and Mammy's too old to have another one. Besides, how would we get it back if it couldn't walk?

'The money's just for expenses,' she explains slowly. 'You wouldn't believe what it costs a lawyer to draw up adoption papers.' She asks questions about what the couple do for a living, whether they've a happy marriage, and whether they're church-goers or not. They always say they are. They think this is the right answer. My Mammy could not give a toss about whether they are Protestants or Roman Catholics or practicing Satanists. She only asks these questions so the whole set-up doesn't sound too suspicious.

'Well,' she says, 'this is an answer to prayer, a real weight off my mind knowing my wee Josh (or Brendan, or Philip) is going to get everything I can't give him. Bless you. Bless you both. Why don't I drop him 'round to youse for a trial run, just for the night? You can see what a wee dote he is and sure, I could lift a deposit off you at the same time, kill two birds with the one stone.'

There is a damp pause. This is the moment when the deal will either take or fail.

'Would five grand seem reasonable?' asks Mammy. Another pause. 'Perfect, I hope you don't mind doing cash. I don't want himself getting at the money. He's a wild man for the drink.'

The deal is all go then. Dad and I do a silent air punch, 'Yesss.' My brother is too young to understand any of this. He thinks it's all just a game, like hide and seek in someone else's house. The people who adopt him will spoil him with ice cream and crisps before bed. They want him to have good memories of his first night in their house. They never think about hiding their iPods or wallets. Why would they suspect a five-year-old child, especially such a cute one? They put him to bed in his new bedroom and don't even notice he's gone till the next morning. My mammy makes Owen leave a note, in crayon, just in case they try to report him missing. This could ruin everything for us.

We've been waiting for over an hour now. I have bit away all the fingernails I can. There's nothing else to do in the dark.

We can't risk the engine. The last thing we need is the neighbours calling the police about a suspicious looking Saxo. Everything rides on a clean getaway, not least my brother, who my parents cannot afford to leave behind. By Mammy's calculations, we need at least two more jobs before we've enough for Australia, especially if we're for taking Owen with us. I'm not that bothered either way. It was better before we got him. There was more room in the back seat for me. My dad had his job at the chicken factory and Mammy made the sort of meals you need both a knife and fork for, not just sandwiches, which we are always having these days.

Everything has changed. We are outlaws now. Mammy has started smoking tight little roll-up cigarettes, which she dangles through a gap in the car window. I am getting fat from all this sitting around, and also the sandwiches. Dad is turning into an American.

I have not seen the jeans jacket in months, but he still insists upon his Bon Jovi tapes. Because my dad was reared in Ballymena, which is a little like being reared in a time machine, he assumes that everyone enjoys Bon Jovi. 'Your love is like bad medicine,' he is singing now. He pauses just long enough to make me think he's forgotten the next line, before he belts out, 'Bad medicine is what I need.' His head is a hammer nodding out each syllable.

There is something about the way my dad taps the beat out

on the steering wheel, prodding at it with a single limp finger, which drives Mammy clean mad. Or, maybe the words are what wind her up. She has never been like bad medicine for Dad, unless Jon Bon Jovi is meaning cough syrup that's gone off. The two of them only touch when they're both going for the TV remote at the same time.

'Turn that shite off, Samuel,' she snaps. 'It's a wonder you've not woken up half the neighbourhood.'

Dad turns the stereo down, a wee bit at first, and then completely off. The car is full of silence and wet breathing. He does this in a way which is meant to make Mammy think he was going to do it anyway.

'Listen,' he says, 'I think I hear a noise.' He rolls the window down a half-inch. Outside the car smells like cut grass and last night's barbecue. 'Naw, it was nothing, just the wind.'

Outside the car is a nice estate of medium-sized houses with pebble-dash walls and two-car driveways. The lawns are perfectly rectangled and green, like the smooth felt on snooker tables. Every third or fourth house has a touring caravan moored outside its garage door. The kind of people who live here are teachers and estate agents or different kinds of social workers. They have two children or three. Sometimes they can't work up to one, and this is where we come in, with my brother.

Experience has taught us that the middling people are more desperate. They are more likely to believe my mammy on the telephone and then, later, at their front door in a dirty T-shirt. They are easier to destroy than the very rich. Very rich people are always suspicious of people who want to help them, even when it is the kind of help they need such as window cleaning or gardening. We only do middle-class houses now. Afterwards, these people are too mortified to call the police. They do not want to look like eejits in front of their friends.

'Besides,' says my mother, 'it's only their holiday savings we've taken or what they were setting aside for a conservatory. They can afford it.'

Every house in the estate has its curtains drawn. Apart from the street lamps and the odd red-eyed alarm, the estate is completely dark. We are parked three houses from the Williamsons', on the opposite side. My brother is inside this house. Any minute now he will turn the key in their patio door and come creeping down the driveway, twisting himself sideways to edge past Mr Williamson's speedboat. His pockets will be full of credit cards and small but valuable items easy to sell on the Internet. Mammy always puts Owen in trousers with deep pockets when he's on a job. She is clever like that, thinking of problems before they happen so they are not even really problems.

'What time is it now, Samuel?' Mammy asks. The digital clock on the Saxo only works when you have the engine on.

Dad tugs at the elbow of his jumper, eases his sleeve off of his watch, and whispers, 'Ten past two, Pearl,' as if someone might be listening outside the door. 'Any minute now, the wee man'll come bolting round yon corner and we'll be out of here.'

We all lean forward, peering through the sweaty windscreen at the street and the hedges and the spot which will, any second now, be Owen, running.

'Next time, I could go,' I suggest.

'No way,' says Mammy, as she always does. In the two seconds it takes to form her next sentence, I tell myself this is because she loves me more than Owen. She is trying to protect me, I tell myself. The believing of this is warm all around me, and spreading out across the back seat, like when you are in the swimmers and allow yourself to piss a little and float in your own heat. Then she says, 'You're too old, Paddy,' and all the good feeling is gone.

'Nobody wants to adopt a ten-year-old,' continues Dad. 'They only go for Owen 'cause he's five and he looks like a wee angel.'

'Like a young Macaulay Culkin,' adds Mammy, 'before he got into the drugs and the sexual stuff. Folks look at that wee face and they can't get their front door open quick enough. The child's a bloody gold mine.'

'Folks look at your face, Paddy, and they go off the idea of children altogether,' says Dad. He winks at me and I can see it, backwards in the rear-view mirror.

'It's not your fault, son,' Mammy butts in. 'You take after your da, not me.'

I bite my teeth into the edge of the passenger seat. It tastes of fire-retardant foam, but it stops me from saying the sort of thing which will land me with a slap. I look over my dad's shoulder while I'm chewing, and I see Owen come belting round the corner in a pair of button-up pyjamas. Everyone springs into action. Dad flicks the ignition on and, for a moment, my brother goes all slow motion, suspended in the Saxo's full beams. Mammy opens the passenger door and jumps out, crying, 'Good lad, Owen,' and, 'What are you in your jammies for?' I get ready to push the passenger seat forward so my brother can get into the back.

Owen stops in front of Mammy. He is close enough to be heard without raising his voice but far enough away to be beyond her reach. I can tell from the way she is holding her arms that she wants to hug him. She is not a very good mammy, but I think she still worries about us, especially Owen, when he's on a job.

'Get in the car, son,' she says.

'Naw, Mammy,' replies my brother, 'I fancy staying with these ones. They're nice.'

'Get in the car, Owen,' she repeats.

My dad leans across the handbrake and shouts, 'Get in the bloody car now, Owen.' He is not even using his John Wayne voice.

'They're going to call me, Miles,' says my brother. 'I've got my own bunk beds: two whole beds and there's only one of me.'

'Get in the car,' all three of us shout.

Mammy makes a lunge for Owen and he stumbles a little trying to avoid her. He is wearing the kind of slippers children wore in wartime. His hair is split in a line down the middle so all his curls are flat.

'I'll skin you, if you don't get in the car right now, Owen,' shouts my dad.

My brother begins to cry, quietly at first and then with a kind of crazy edge like an out-of-control truck thundering down a hill. A light goes on in the house closest to us.

'I don't want to do the stealing any more,' screams Owen. He does not look like a young Macaulay Culkin now. He looks like a just-born baby all pink-faced and screaming. 'It's not fair. Why doesn't Paddy have to do it?'

'I will,' I say, 'I'll totally do it.'

Nobody hears me. Mammy takes three steps towards my brother. She wraps her arms around his arms and braces him against her chest as if he was a sack of new potatoes. She throws him in the back seat and does not even bother with his seatbelt.

'Drive,' she says to Dad, and neither of them bother with their seatbelts either.

'I could make myself look younger than I am,' I say. 'I could wear, like, a Disney jumper or something.'

'Wee bugger didn't even lift a credit card,' my mammy mumbles to herself.

'At least we've got the deposit,' says Dad. They both turn their heads to look at the glove compartment where Mammy has stashed six grand in fifty-pound notes.

'He's getting too old for this, Samuel.'

'We only need him to do it two more times.'

'You're right, two more jobs, and then Australia.'

'And if worst comes to worst, Pearl, I can always take my belt to him – for his own good.'

In the back seat, my brother is still crying. He reaches through the dark for my hand, and I will not take it.

'You could have stayed with them,' I hiss in his ear. I hate my brother for coming back to the Saxo, for still being the one they need.

In the front, my dad has turned the radio back on and it is Bon Jovi, the one about saying a prayer. I think this is their most famous song.

7.

More of a Handstand Girl

My brother is allergic to people. He lives in the spare-room closet. It is four years, two months and a handful of days since I last saw his face. It is no big deal. He is not my twin brother. I am a girl and I am not allergic to people. I like people just fine.

My brother is allergic to people. He told me this one night, ten days after he first moved into the spare-room closet. I thought it was just an adolescent phase. He was odd and determined, utterly set on living inside a closet.

He moved the stereo into the closet and ran an extension lead to the nearest outlet. I made him ready meals and peanut-butter sandwiches, leaving them on a tray with eating instructions just outside his door. It was the best of times. I felt useful, like a real girl. Even then I couldn't see his face. He wore a motorcycle helmet every time he crossed the hall to the bathroom. I took to wearing dark glasses inside. I pretended I couldn't see him. It was important to indulge him.

I was on the other side of the apartment when my brother first told me about his allergy. We were talking into two Campbell's soup cans attached by a piece of string. They still smelt of mushroom soup when you raised them to your mouth for speaking.

'Don't lick the edges of the telephone,' I said, because my brother, when he was younger, had liked to lick things such as coins and forks in restaurants.

'Don't be stupid,' he said. 'I only lick things I like.'

My brother has never liked mushrooms.

I was watching television in the front room, describing everything I could see through my dark glasses, laughing into the soup can so the laugh went jiggling all the way down the string into my brother's ear. There was no television in the spare-room closet.

Between the programmes there was a commercial for hay-fever remedy. 'Hey,' I said to my brother at the other end of the Campbell's-soup-can phone, 'Remember the time our mom got hay fever?'

My brother remembered that whole crazy summer like it was only yesterday or the day before. He remembered the way our mom used to tape a Kleenex across her mouth and nose to filter out the pollen. We talked about the way those Kleenexes rose and fell with every breath, like tiny parachutes descending on her face. My brother remembered the acupuncture, and the time our mother set fire to the neighbours' herb garden. In fact, my brother accurately remembered almost every detail of that whole hay-fever summer, and so, naturally, we got to talking about allergies.

I said, 'I guess I'm allergic to this dumb city. I guess I've almost caught asthma from it.' I huffed on an empty inhaler to prove my point.

'That's nothing,' my brother replied. 'I am allergic to people. If someone sees me I might probably die. I might probably die the kind of violent death where I have to go to hospital immediately even though everyone knows it is already too late.'

I knew exactly the kind of death he was talking about. I watch a lot of television in my spare time.

I stopped considering the spare-room closet an adolescent phase and became very serious about my brother's condition. 'Listen here,' I said in a very serious voice, though I could never be sure how well my vocal inflections were travelling down the Campbell's-soup-can phone, 'we've got to be very serious about your condition. This is no laughing matter. At any minute you might probably die.'

My brother agreed wholeheartedly. I could hear him nodding down the telephone string.

Right after this conversation I built a trash-bag wall between my brother and I. I split the apartment in two and drew a map to avoid confusion. I am good with lines and other straight things. 'That is your side and this is mine,' I shouted through the trash-bag wall. Everything was plastic and futuristic like the part in *ET* where the science people try to steal ET and do experiments on him. My brother used to cry at that part in the movie. It was sadder to him than the time our grandma really died.

Building those black plastic walls down the middle of our apartment, I felt older and clever, like a scientist.

We got a bathroom each, and I got the television. 'What about the kitchen?' my brother asked and I got it because I am the girl and I am entirely capable of sliding his meals under the trash bag every morning and evening.

'It works,' he said. I imagined it was the last conversation we'd ever have.

I wrote his words on a Post-it note and stuck them to the fridge. 'It works.' Last words are important things, not to be forgotten.

It is four years, two months and a handful of days since I last saw my brother's face. His allergy has gotten worse. Just thinking about people is enough to bring him out in hives all the way down his back. He tells me this, whispering into the soup-can phone late at night. We don't speak now. If I hold my breath and keep the line quiet, he can pretend I don't even exist. He can imagine an apartment at the end of the world where he is the only real person left. He can tell himself, 'This isn't my sister. This isn't a telephone. This isn't even a conversation. It's just the only boy in the world talking to himself, cramming all his thoughts into a Campbell's-condensed-soup can.'

If I don't breathe and I don't speak and I manage not to jiggle the soup-can string, he feels completely alone and the hives are barely visible.

Lately my brother has begun a new project. He is building himself a suit of armour which will protect him from all the people who might probably kill him.

The real suit of armour will take months and months, possibly years to be finished. However, my brother is building practise armour out of tinfoil. He tapes the tinfoil to his body with Scotch tape and gathers the ankles and wrists together with elastic bands. He wears mismatched oven mitts on his hands. The thumb is in the wrong place on the left. He wears my father's old fishing boots on his feet and the motorcycle helmet up top.

'I wish you could see me,' he says, whispering into the Campbell's-soup-can phone, 'I look just like an astronaut in my armour.'

This is a dumb thing for my brother to say. He has not yet tested out the armour. If someone sees him at this stage he might probably die.

My brother practises on next door's kitten, which is now a cat.

He stands in the middle of the spare room wearing his tinfoil armour and makes the noise which attracts cats. My mother, before she went up in flames, told me that people in France make a different noise to attract cats. If this is true I find it very intriguing. It means that animals can speak in foreign languages and that is a very interesting idea to consider. However, having known my mother in the years before she went up in flames, it is more than likely bullshit.

My brother practises being seen with next door's cat. He stands in the middle of the spare room, wearing his tinfoil armour and forces the cat to look straight at him. He does not come out in hives. The tinfoil armour is an all round success, though not very practical, as it rips every time he takes a step.

'Back to the drawing board,' my brother mutters down the Campbell's-soup-can phone, but he sounds happy.

One Sunday afternoon, my brother practised on next door's cat without his tinfoil armour. Afterwards he told me all about it. The experiment was not a success. My brother only got as far as removing the tinfoil arms and his left leg before the hives started and he began to probably die so quickly he had to hide in the spare-room closet for three hours. It was a close call. It took two weeks for my brother to fully recover. But he did recover. My brother has always been odd and determined, as was my mother who'd been vowing to go up in flames for years before she finally managed it.

Last weekend I saw my brother climbing the fire escape outside the spare-room window, stark naked with only the roof-top pigeons to watch his progress. Pausing halfway up the ladder, he scattered huge handfuls of breadcrumbs into the night sky while the pigeons swooped and dived and saw him in all his milk-white glory. I said nothing, following his logic from a distance. Being seen by a pigeon is a hell of a lot less like being seen by a real person than next door's cat. There were no repercussions to the whole pigeon experiment. Perhaps my brother is recovering from his very serious condition.

I said nothing. If my brother knew I had seen him stark naked on the fire escape, the chances are he might probably have died.

The real suit of armour is well under way now.

I steal knives and forks for him, fine cutlery from the street cafés outside our apartment. I carry a huge bag every time I leave the apartment. My mother used to keep all her wigs in this bag. It is big enough to hide next door's cat and two other cats beside, should I ever have the inclination. I steal almost everything that isn't pinned down.

I am like a magpie. I'm particularly drawn to shiny things.

I steal knives and forks, biscuit-tin lids, hubcaps from the cars which park in the side streets behind our apartment, bicycle chains, scissors, nails and screws right out of peoples' doors. I steal earrings and necklaces from the department stores in the city centre. I'll steal anything made of metal. I shrink my lungs down into my stomach and do my youngest, smallest face so no one will notice me. Then I slide things into my enormous bag and run all the way home to our apartment.

I have never been caught.

Perhaps I am very good at stealing and this is why I have never been caught. Perhaps it is because I only steal things which no one else wants.

My brother once said to me, 'You should read *Oliver Twist* by Charles Dickens because it is about children who steal things. Maybe you will get some tips.'

What a good idea, I thought. The very next day I stole the *Oliver Twist* book from the downtown library. It was the only non-metallic thing I've ever stolen. I read it cover to cover in less than two days and wished I hadn't bothered. I learnt nothing new from *Oliver Twist*. The words were old-fashioned and gave me a migraine headache.

My brother keeps me up late with the banging.

Somewhere on the other side of the trash-bag wall he is building a beautiful thing: a shiny, shiny suit of armour which will keep him safe every time he might probably die. I dream that suit of armour like you would not believe. I dream that all the banging, all the soldering and spoons, hubcaps and bicycle chains will build me a new brother: a seven-foot-tall brother with iron lungs and a silver smile. I dream a brother who might probably never die, who will climb fire escapes late at night and shine like a constellation prize. I dream a golden brother who no longer lives in the spare-room closet, a brother who works properly.

The banging stops. It is 4:30 in the morning.

'Picture this,' my real brother says, humming down the Campbell's-soup-can phone, 'I have robot arms and robot legs. I sing like a wristwatch when I walk. I am, all but my feet, invincible now.'

I am happy for him in his biscuit-tin suit, smiling over his soldering irons with a seven-inch zip for a mouth. And, I am at the same time sad for his real-boy face, which I can never again see, and his skin, which is halfway freckled on both cheeks, exactly like mine.

Sometimes I am lonely, like a real girl should be. I whisper the loneliness into the Campbell's-soup-can phone, early in the morning when I am sure my brother will be asleep.

I know all the boys in our apartment block. I bring them home and stick them like Band-Aids on the loneliness.

'Ignore the cat,' I say, 'and the banging. It's only my brother who might probably die if anyone sees him.'

They think I am crazy, like my mother who went up in flames, leaving a charred spot on the living-room floor. I serve them root beer in tall glasses and turn cartwheels across the floorboards.

'Ignore the banging,' I say. 'Watch my legs make distractions in the air.'

I strip down to my underwear and turn cartwheels up and down the living-room floor while the boys drink root beer and look nervously at the charred place where my mother went up in flames.

I never tell the truth. I have always been more of a handstand girl, but these days it smarts to stand still.

The banging persists, sharking under the trash-bag curtain. The boys get nervous. They look at their watches and check their cell phones for a getaway plan. I take both my arms and tie them to the living-room sofa. I turn more cartwheels and the cartwheels are secret code for, 'Do not leave me. I am lonely with my brother who cannot be seen and the charred place where my mother went up in flames. Drink my root beer and talk to me like a real boy with a mouth that moves. Watch detective shows on cable. Bitch about the beautiful girls from the year above.'

The banging persists. The boys get nervous. My mouth will not move honestly without a Campbell's-soup-can phone.

I hold their knees and say, 'I am very good at doing sex, you know.'

All the boys in our apartment block want to hear this, but none of them know how to respond. They strip down to their underwear and turn cartwheels across the living room floor, avoiding the charred place where my mother went up in flames, and though I am more of a handstand girl, even this is better than silence. When the banging grows too cymbal-sharp to ignore, they leave through the front door.

They stop at every apartment on our floor and say, 'It's so sad. Those kids are crazy. We should send round Social Services, or a chicken casserole.' They do not mention the cartwheels or the rings, and chains, the belt buckles, braces and earrings they have paid for the privilege of being with me.

I am lonely like a houseplant, practicing my handstands against the bathroom door.

The armour is almost done.

At night my brother wears the motorcycle helmet and we talk. As long as he keeps the motorcycle helmet on, we can have real conversations, pulling our sentences backwards and forwards across our Campbell's-soup-can phones. We talk about the ever after. We talk about taking a vacation in a dry place; New Mexico is always an option. We talk about asking for help and always agree to talk more at a later date.

God is on our side. We asked him specially and he slept on it for three days, rising on the third to say, 'Yes, yes and yes again.' We are still his children and we are glad like you would not believe. We write our gladness in the margarine tub with butter knives and baby fingers, passing the margarine like secret messages backwards and forwards beneath the trash-bag wall. God is on our side, giving us good things: coupons for free fries at McDonald's, next door's kitten, the perfect imprint of a dead moth on the bathroom tiles, a mother who left before she could do any real damage.

We do not talk about our mother now. I avoid the charred place in the living room where she went up in flames and her closet, which still smells like hairspray and dime-store soap. I drink her vodka and throw her records from the open windows and pretend like she never asked for children made in her own image. Every morning I watch my face in the bathroom mirror. I am becoming her, woebegone eyebrows and all. I pinch my cheeks and fold my nose. I suck my lips till they bleed carnation pink.

I say, 'We are not our mother. We will not go up in flames nor disappear with the sadness.'

On very good mornings, the days when we have pancakes, I almost believe myself.

The banging is much slower these days. The armour is almost finished.

I ask my brother when he will be done.

'Soon,' he says.

Soon is not a year or months from now. Soon is Tuesday evening at six o'clock, after *Quincy* and a microwaved lasagne.

'It works,' my brother says. Last words and first words, smiling down the Campbell's-soup-can phone. 'Even my feet are invincible now. I have practised on next door's cat and a whole host of unsuspecting pigeons. I am ready to come out of the spare-room closet.'

My brother comes out, ripping the trash-bag curtain from side to side in one huge metallic swoop. He stands before me, seven feet tall in his silver boots. He is an astronaut, a robot, a golden calf waiting to topple over. He is half blind with the glare and accidentally steps in the charred place where our mother went up in flames. I wonder if he can feel her sadness seeping all the way through his robot shoes.

I reach out one finger and trace the outline of a dinner fork across the left side of his belly. He feels nothing. I pin fridge magnets to his back. He feels nothing. I beat him over the head with a fish slice and an industrial-sized whisk. He feels nothing, only registering the dull clunk of metal on insulated metal.

I say, 'Can you see me seeing you? Do you still think you might probably die if I see you?'

He says nothing.

I push the Campbell's-soup-can phone against the side of his motorcycle-helmet head and repeat my question, yelling so loud that next door's cat retreats to the safety of the fire escape.

No response, but I think he's smiling.

I strip down to my underwear and turn cartwheels all across the living room floor even though I know it's wrong. My brother stands right there by the coffee table, beaming like a television antenna. He is shiny and useless, safe as cabbage. He might probably never die and I am mad like you would not believe.

I let my brother stand for three weeks straight. He has not yet chanced the world outside our apartment door. He sleeps standing up in his armour and eats through a tiny tube attached to the motorcycle helmet. I liquidise everything, even his root beer, and pour the liquids into his head as if he is a potted plant.

I imagine my brother is disappearing inside his armour and no amount of cartwheels will bring him back.

I am lonely like my lungs are falling out. I have no friends my own age, even the boys from our apartment block no longer believe me when I say, 'I am very good at doing sex.' I have nothing left to steal and no one to hold still for. I watch detective shows on cable and sleep with one arm around next door's kitten, who is now a cat and squeals loudly at my advances, preferring anyone's arms to mine, even my mechanical brother's.

When the loneliness gets too loud to swallow, I take a tin opener and slice my brother wide open in his sleep. I see him. He is milk-white under the metal. His arms and legs are the colour of frozen sausages. I see him for thirty minutes, a whole half hour of seeing. I know that he might probably die now, but I cannot quit seeing.

Nothing happens. My brother sleeps like a baby, unaware of the seeing and the wide metal gash splicing him open as if he was a tin of beans. I can almost see his insides.

I go sit in the charred place on the living room floor. I think about going up in flames and my eyebrows are already there.

8.

Contemporary Uses for a Belfast Box Room

Box room: A room or cupboard used for storing miscellaneous articles, too good to be thrown out or given away, which may be useful at some future time.

One: Least-Favourite Child

When the second child arrived – sky-eyed and abundantly blond, with a keen, Northern wit already peaking – the first child lost its appeal.

'What's the point of it?' they asked, turning the first child backwards and forwards like long division on the living room rug. 'It's not particularly bonny. It doesn't speak. It can't even stand up without the assistance of furniture.'

'It costs money,' they agreed and suspected it was not worth the investment.

'I'd have preferred a boat,' he admitted. She had thoughts of en-suite bathrooms and Continental holidays, unmentioned.

Though no one, not even the lady doctor, had thought to warn them, they soon discovered it was almost impossible to return a child, once opened.

'But this isn't what we ordered,' they'd explained, hanging on the hospital telephone till the pips dripped feebly into the middle distance. 'It doesn't even understand English. Can't we get a different one?'

The hospital had other things to be getting on with: genuine emergencies and two-car pile-ups, a harrowing bed shortage in the A & E. 'It could be worse,' snapped the lady doctor. 'We might have given you a pair.' She hung up before they could petition the managing director.

They shrugged their disappointment and installed the first child in the spare bedroom, where it fussed and fell over and could not be coerced into polite conversation, even after several glasses of red.

They were not deliberately cruel. They tolerated the child's presence at meals and in short, social bursts during the space between one television programme and the next. Three weeks after its arrival they gave it a name. Yet, from time to time, rising in the night to fill and empty the child, they could recall neither its given name nor a single significant feature which might set it apart from other more useful household appliances.

The second child was Christmas in comparison.

She arrived with a name, with a bright academic future and advanced conversational skills. They couldn't have been more delighted. Their only regret was a niggling suspicion that they should have ordered two. Accustomed to measuring their concern in small, dutiful teaspoons, they were surprised to find themselves capable of spades, buckets and a tremendous landsliding love.

'Surely,' they said, setting the first child against its secondary sibling, 'anyone with an eye in his head would favour the new one.'

The second child beamed back at them, a mirror for their worst and best. The first child, rising in its own defence, reached for a kindly piece of furniture and, finding that even the coffee table had now turned its wooden back, fell flatly upon its own unremarkable arse.

Thus convinced, they moved the first child into the box room and installed the second in the spare bedroom.

When visitors and close family friends enquired about this odd arrangement, pointing out that surely the first child, by nature of birth, deserved the spare room, they could barely muster a contrite blush.

'The second one's our favourite,' they stated boldly. 'She deserves plenty of room to grow.'

In time they proved themselves entirely justified, for the first child, constricted by the boots, the suitcases and paperback novels which had accumulated in the box room, never grew long or loud enough to defend its own birthright.

Two: Storing Poets

After six years, he realised that the novel was going nowhere. Where he'd hoped for a final, pointed full stop, self-indulgence had unleashed subplots, appendices and a whole swooning troop of half-boiled sentiments.

At cocktail parties and funerals, he quit calling himself a 'novelist', then a 'writer' and finally could not think of anything to call himself, and hung like a pair of inconspicuous curtains by the refreshments table. He came to despise words and, having never fully trusted numbers, wondered if there were jobs which might require no constructive thought: professional athletics perhaps, or deep-sea diving. On the night before Halloween, he dreamt himself a plumber's assistant and woke happier than a hothouse flower.

'It's only paper,' he said and felt confident that it could be made to disappear, individual sheets and sentences disintegrating until it was no longer a mountain but rather the ghost of an avalanche, avoided.

The following morning he confronted his wife over breakfast.

'Darling,' he said, and could tell she was immediately suspicious, 'after the weekend I'm going to get a proper job and no longer be a novelist.'

'What about the book?' his wife asked, stirring her breakfast cereal to mush and mumbling nonsense in order to keep her anger occupied.

'There's nothing in it. Nothing worth keeping anyway.'

'But it's enormous,' cried his wife, pointing to the towering stacks of foolscap, like Babel, nestling in all four corners of the dining room. 'We haven't had room for anything else.'

Silence settled over the breakfast table as they considered all the specific examples of everything else which had fallen victim to the book.

'Dinner parties,' he confessed apologetically.

'Hobbies,' she mumbled. 'Sewing, for example, and possibly gardening.'

'The loft extension.'

'Summer holidays.'

'Babies,' they both agreed, though her voice was barely audible behind his.

When their losses had been lined up like fine cutlery, it

seemed a terrible waste to disregard all those words, all those bloated sentences and paragraphs.

'What about poetry?' his wife suggested. 'It's smaller but it's still made of words.'

And, because he did not want to disappoint her again, twice in a matter of meals, he agreed to try poems

After breakfast he kissed his wife on the lobe of each ear and finally on the forehead; she was prettier when he could not see her face.

'Throw the novel in the recycling bin,' he said with forced bravado, 'see if it comes back as a dictionary or something useful. I am a much diminished man.'

The box room beckoned. Once the patio furniture had been evicted, the space was perfectly adequate for a poet of limited ambition. He locked the door, double-barred himself against claustrophobia and, snug as a wool-knit sweater, wondered why he'd bothered with anything as Continental as a novel. The box room shrunk in approval, demanding clipped thoughts, neatly written. The ceiling pressed for concision, the walls constricted, too tight to tolerate anything bigger than a medium-sized sonnet. In the corner by the radiator, the vacuum cleaner hovered, ready to devour every wasteful word.

For company, he kept a Moleskine notebook and a sharpened pencil. For food, he starved. For inspiration, he lay on the carpet and watched the summer jets ascending and descending the city airport like wide-winged, tropical fish floating in the box room's skylight.

On the fifth day, his wife beat the door down with the blunt end of a steam iron. She found him greatly reduced and grinning like a television set.

'I've written a poem,' he said, thrusting the Moleskine under her nose. 'It's everything I've ever wanted to say.'

She took the notebook from his hands and flicked from front to back, finding no stanza, no sentence, no single, sharpish word upon which to hang a compliment.

'The box room helped,' he admitted, flinging his arms as wide as the walls would allow. 'There's no room for self-indulgence here.'

She stared at him, frowning as she paged the notebook slowly, finding nothing more than a single, concisely printed letter 'A'; perhaps this was the beginning of everything else.

Three: Hobbies

'Perfect for a home office,' explained the estate agent, opening the door to reveal a space roughly the shape and size of a disabled toilet. 'It's amazing what you can do with shelves.'

'Ikea,' replied his wife, knowingly. He was unsure if this was a question or an answer, but was certain that they did not require a home office, and said as much, forcefully.

'Room for a baby?' suggested the estate agent. 'If you don't have one, you could get one now you've got somewhere to put it.'

He answered with great conviction on behalf of his five children (already planted in several cities), and his wife (the third and youngest of his three), who was clouding over, threatening rain at the first mention of babies, and also his own fragile wit, which was too old and life-dull for the joy that such things required.

He glared at the estate agent. His mouth said, 'No thanks.' His eyebrows, pitched in furious consternation, said, 'Look what you've done,' and 'Have a bleeding heart,' and, 'Don't be opening that barrel of monkeys, mate.'

'A great wee space for hobbies,' suggested the estate agent somewhat desperately. 'Do you have any hobbies, sir?'

In the moment he could only recall whiskey, football and last summer's fleeting affair with the golf course, none of which could be coerced up the poky staircase to settle in a space less than two metres square. His wife's eyes were already turning bloodshot blue, her nose blurring in the familiar fashion. 'Allotments,' he said, with hurtling enthusiasm, 'I've always wanted an allotment but there's a terrible waiting list for the ones down by the embankment. This space would be perfect, don't you think, sweetheart?'

It was a brute lie. All three knew it, but bound by the walls and the thin air staling around them, they would believe any fool thing for a fire escape.

'We'll take it,' he said, and within a week he was ploughing up the carpet, planting carrots and tiny seedling potatoes in perpendicular drills. After Christmas, he hoped to plant flowers and strawberries in individual grow bags. Originally he'd planned on tomatoes, but his wife was afraid they'd stink the place out with their green, metallic smell.

He carried a kitchen chair up the stairs, installed it in the corner with car magazines and a thermos flask and never felt quite comfortable in his own space.

'He's so happy in his allotment,' his wife told her girlfriends. 'Most evenings he's just up there pottering away. It keeps him out from under my feet. The allotment's the best thing that ever happened to us.'

No one believed his wife. She no longer believed herself and did not care so long as the friends continued to come and go, drinking her coffee and occasionally laughing, never once asking how she really, honestly was.

Upstairs in the box room the walls began to fur. His beard grew out in sympathy. He no longer recognised himself in the bathroom mirror. The plants, sensing his desperation, refused to sprout.

He tried new tricks, stolen from the Internet. He spread manure, thick as cottage cheese, over the topsoil, drifting in and out of consciousness on its meaty stench. Occasionally he sang. He kept the curtains closed for heat and tacked black bin liners across the windowpanes. The sprouts failed and the cabbages were sprouts, barely bigger than his thumbnail.

He lit the room by means of Christmas lights and a carefully strung network of desk lamps. He played records, purposefully selecting softer tracks: ballads and love songs which might coerce the smaller shoots into peaking. Nothing grew.

He fed the plants daily, a measured blend of whiskey, water and his own sodden rage. The plants drowned, permeating the floor to leave drip marks on the ceiling below.

'Your allotment's leaking,' his wife pointed out, barely lifting her head from the breakfast cereal. He willed her to suggest another hobby – embroidery, stamp collecting, basket weaving – anything which would not feel like a door had closed firmly between them. But she said nothing as she helped him place buckets and saucepans beneath the worst of the drips.

Later he would find things buried in the allotment: baby shoes, a teething ring, two dozen nappies still packaged. Holding them to the light he could no longer recall if these sadnesses had been planted or had sprouted unbidden like weeds in an untended field.

9.

Swept

There were six brown leaves and an empty Twix wrapper lying outside their door. It was only the third week of August. June hadn't been expecting leaves yet.

'Will you look at that,' she said, retracting the venetian blinds to give Bill a better view, 'there's leaves on the doorstep already and it's not even September.'

Bill lowered the *News Letter* and slipped his reading glasses from the bridge of his nose to the front of his forehead, where they spent most of their time, scrutinising the ceiling. It was almost five minutes since he'd last read a sentence, though he was anxious to preserve the illusion of reading. Since his retirement, a frugal half hour with the paper was his only respite from June's hovering attention. He was loath to compromise his own alibi.

June was a tiny teaspoon of a woman. The whole of her, sitting down, could fold into the space between Bill's armpit and his arse. In the past he'd liked to sit like this on the living-room sofa, two jigsaw pieces perfectly fitted, watching the telly or asking the homely questions which bridged the hour between dinner and bed:

'How was work?'

'Did you get out of the house at all today?'

'Anything strange or startling with yourself?'

Their answers could be copied and pasted from one evening to the next but it was a liturgy of sorts, to ask and be answered and almost always (except on Saturdays and Sundays), make tentative plans for the weekend: roast beef and a run to Bangor, her mother, his sister, a Chinese on Saturday night. Bill had always found something to look forward to in a weekend.

In the past, Bill had liked June best in these moments, tucked into his side like an Icarus wing, her words catching in his beard, condensing to form a warm, mumbling fug. He'd understood her completely even when he could not hear her. Her hair had not been permed then. It would crease against his face like embroidery silk and smelt of Vosene shampoo. While Vosene smelt crisp and medical on him, on June the same smell was Glenariff forest, and two nights before Christmas, the good soap his mother kept for visitors and family wakes.

In the past, Bill had left June and returned to find her still there, each evening, in the kitchen, not so much diminished as unknown. Every day, he'd taken great trouble to forget her whilst he worked, allowing the cut of her heels and the crush of her smile to slip down the back of his mind like loose change or paper clips. Each evening, the rediscovery of June, just as he'd forgotten her, was delicious.

Now Bill never left and June did not know how to leave, so there could be no returning. The house, which had, for eighteen or more years, quite comfortably accommodated two adults, three children and a rolling cast of incidentals, now seemed as tight as a two-day toothache. Everywhere Bill turned, June was already there, and on the other three sides were walls.

She liked having him around.

She'd waited years to have him all to herself.

She told him so much, every night over dinner eaten off a tray. She could not contain her contentment on the telephone to friends.

Bill felt like a thing you bought in a shop and kept on the mantelpiece. He hated the way June looked at him. There was no lust left in her, no mystery, nor fear that he might leave and never come back, only a clutching need to know where he was from one moment to the next. There was nowhere Bill could go to get away from her. The house was soldered to the house next door on both sides and did not have a garden. Even in the downstairs toilet with the door double-barred June pestered him with questions about the hand towels, and the soap, and his bowels, which were not as reliable as they'd once been and could not be doing with any undue harassment.

He still loved her, of course. He was too old to consider adapting his palate to another woman's cooking and June was in better shape than most of his friends' wives. She wasn't doting and she'd not gone religious. Her legs were still roughly the shape that legs should be and when she wore her 'going out' pants, the spare flesh around her belly could be coerced back into something approximating the waistline he'd fallen in love with. Best of all, there was a particular spot on the back of her neck which had proven impervious to the aging process and still touched, tasted and smelt exactly as it had in 1965. For these and other meagre mercies, Bill was grateful. Yet he could not help but wish his wife would go away for most of every day and sometimes weekends.

Bill took every opportunity to leave. The door was the obvious route, but half a dozen tins of Tennent's, consumed in quick succession, could provide the same result without requiring him to leave the sofa. Bill took every opportunity to leave, but it was not the same as before. There was nowhere to go and he knew he'd always come back.

Though he'd never been much of a newspaper man he began to relish his morning walk, up the Cregagh Road to the newsagent, for a *News Letter* and a jumbo Twix. He ate both bars on a bench outside the Post Office and, afterwards, licked the chocolate from his fingers lest June read rebellion in the spots where the Twix had melted onto his hands. He liked a Twix on weekdays and a Galaxy Caramel at the weekend and could neither explain nor understand this preference. June no longer tolerated biscuits or chocolate bars. She'd read an article about cholesterol in *Take a Break* magazine and had ever since outlawed chocolate, full-fat milk and proper butter. Bill had lost three pounds in the first week of June's new regime and four in the second. Terrified that he might disappear altogether, he'd begun to buy, and con-sume, a jumbo Twix every time he left the house. Sustenance, he called it, when in reality he knew it was nothing short of mutiny. Sometimes, for sheer wickedness, Bill carried his Twix wrapper home and dropped it outside their front door. There was a deep pleasure, distinct and separate to consuming the chocolate, in the knowledge that this small act of selfishness would irritate June immensely.

Each time Bill felt guilty about littering, he considered the tub of Flora margarine which had, of late, ousted the comforting little brick of Golden Cow butter from his fridge door. He felt justified and inclined to spit when he dropped the next wrapper. It was easy to irritate June. She'd been raised pernickety by a woman who ironed hankies and dried her tea bags in the hot press.

Bill had never hit his wife or even come close. He was not a cruel man, nor violent, and could not stand deliberate cruelty in others. However, as he approached his second year of retirement, the desire to make June's life as tight and miserable as she'd made

his, became one of his few remaining pleasures. He left the back
door open and never replaced the toilet roll in either bathroom.
He watched Sky Sports with the volume turned up and shoved
used tissues down the side of the sofa. He dropped many small
items of litter on their front doorstep, sometimes lifting things
from the kitchen bin just to deposit them outside. These empty
crisp bags and packets were not so much rebellion as love letters
to the women June had once been, crumpled calls to clash and
argue and reconcile as they'd once reconciled, furiously, with arms
and teeth.

June never once linked Bill to the litter. She blamed the postman and the gang of young lads in tracksuits who lingered at the
end of their street, huddled and whooping like old-time evangel-
ists. She blamed the Polish family who'd moved in two doors up,
on the other side. Bill realised that she no longer believed him
capable of rebellion. Today, as he observed his wife over the top
of the farming supplement, Bill finally admitted that there was
very little left of June to like. He wondered, as he often wondered,
if she was as disappointed as he was.

'There's leaves everywhere out there,' she said, louder now,
for she could tell Bill wasn't really listening, 'and some dirty
fecker's dropped a Twix wrapper at their backside. I'm going to
have to sweep up. I don't want the house looking like a tip when
Maureen arrives.'

'No point bothering yourself,' muttered Bill. 'Your Maureen'll
be quick enough to find fault whether you clean the place or not.'

June's sister, Maureen was expected from Lisburn on the bus,
sometime between four and five. She visited twice a year for no
reason, and once again on Boxing Day. Lately, since the kids had
left home and Bill retired, these visits had come to pass for
occasions, thinly anticipated blips in the boredom of their everyday routine. In preparation for her arrival, Bill had repainted the

downstairs toilet. June had baked three dozen shortbread and changed the spare-bedroom sheets on the off-chance that Maureen might take the head staggers, accept more than her usual half-glass of sherry, and be persuaded to stay the night.

Bill could not bear Maureen. He dreaded her visits and could barely stomach her from the far side of the room at family occasions. She was older than June, pinchy in appearance and demeanour. She'd never approved of her sister's choice in husbands and while she'd yet to vocalise her opinions, there was something in the way she left and entered Bill's house which made her disapproval quite clear.

'She thinks you're common,' June had explained to Bill on their honeymoon night after his new sister-in-law had spent the afternoon frowning at him from beneath the shadowy brim of her wedding hat. Maureen had, it was noted by more than one guest, worn the same dress to June's wedding as she'd worn earlier in the year to their late grandmother's funeral. 'She thinks I could have done better,' June continued. 'She'd have liked me to marry a Presbyterian. Church of Ireland's a bit papish in her book.'

At first he'd thought June was joking, but as she stepped from the en-suite into the thankless light of their bedroom, Bill noticed that his wife was on the verge of tears.

Everything in him rose in rage and, had the sister-in-law been with them, there in the tiny hotel room still wearing her funeral frock, he would have thundered and struck her hard enough to leave a mark. Instead, he'd picked June up by her tight-laced waist and carried her across the hotel room, gentle as a vase of shop-bought flowers. As her shoes peeled loose and her braids unwound, he flung her across the bed and she bounced, once, twice, three times like a skimming stone before coming to rest against the pillows. 'I'll show you just how common I can be,' he cried, and hadn't even bothered with the buttons on her wedding dress. It was a clumsy attempt to make light of the situation, but neither party felt particularly light. Maureen's disapproval hung like a cloud canopy over their wedding bed, persisting all the way through the honeymoon until, on the third morning, June finally broke the familial ranks.

'My sister's an awful bitch, so she is.'

And Bill had felt for the first time, complicit, as if a line had been crossed and all necessary leaving and cleaving was now complete. Tempting her resolve, he'd asked, 'You still love her though, don't you, pet?' and was justified when she answered quickly and earnestly, 'Course, but not as much as I love you, Billy.'

At the time, this had pleased Bill immensely, but the threat of Maureen seemed to smoulder on the edge of his marriage like a downpour predicted for the day after tomorrow. It was a war of sorts, with Bill in one corner and Maureen in the other, poor neutral June in the middle dragged this way and that like a Swiss saint. What to do about Christmas? Should their dad go into a nursing home, and if so, which one? Who was to have Mother's Country Rose? Maureen had strong opinions on every topic. Bill differed vehemently. June could not have cared less either way, so long as everyone kept from yelling.

Bill's sister-in-law had always reminded him of a cartoon skeleton his kids liked to watch on children's programmes. The children agreed with him. June said this was unfair and unnecessarily cruel in light of the cancer. June said the cancer had made her sister mean, but the cancer was a relatively new excuse and could not stand against well-documented accounts of Maureen's meanness stretching right back to 1957. June always defended her sister, even when she forgot the children's birthdays and mixed them up with her nieces and nephews on the other side.

'Your Aunty Maureen's been through a lot.' June would argue.

'She'd had the cancer and lost two husbands before her sixtieth. It's no joke. You should all be nicer to her.'

The children would nod reverently. They loved their mother without qualm or question but had very little regard for her sister. Early on they'd learnt not to expect much from Aunty Maureen. Whilst their other aunts and grandparents distributed £5 notes for birthdays and selection boxes for Christmas, they were lucky to get 20 pence in a card from Maureen and, like as not, to receive a Bible-verse bookmark instead. As soon as they were old enough to lower their expectations, they quit hoping for material gain from Aunty Maureen and began to appreciate her as a never-ending source of comedy material. They were not bad children, but all of them, even the one who ended up in politics, had inherited Bill's wicked sense of humour.

'Aye, but admit it, Mum,' his youngest would always fire back, each time June tried to defend her sister, 'she does look a bit like Skeletor, doesn't she?'

June tried to remain stern whilst she grinned into the back of her hand, the corners of her mouth peeking like latitudinal creases from behind her fingers. Bill would be certain in these moments that she was 'one of them' now, grafted onto and loyal to their own little tribe. If forced to choose, she would pick him and their children again and again, even on the worst days. This realisation allowed Bill to tolerate Maureen at Christmas and funerals and twice a year, for no particular reason.

Lately however, Bill had found it harder and harder to stomach the idea of Maureen, even in small helpings. The more June irritated him, the less grace he had for her sister. This evening he knew there would be dinner at the table and tea in cups with matching saucers. June would fuss and flap like a nervous pigeon, up and down the stairs, moving ornaments half an inch to the left or right. Later, he'd find himself trapped in his own living room with not one, but two elderly ladies, talking about people he didn't know. None of this appealed to Bill, even the eating parts.

He lifted his eyes from the farming section. June was working her way across the individual slats of the venetian blinds with a wad of cotton wool. She had her slippers on with her outdoor clothes, and Bill saw her, for a moment, as strangers might see her if she were a character on a television drama. She was not someone he'd wish to meet if they'd not already been married.

'Uch, quit fussing, June,' he muttered. 'Sure, it's only your sister.'

'And my sister will notice every wee speck of dust and hold it against me from now till kingdom come. You could eat your dinner off her front doorstep, Bill, and take your tea from her toilet bowl.'

'And much happiness all that cleaning has done her.'

June didn't seem to hear, or chose not to hear. She plumped the cushions on the Chesterfield, working around the spot where Bill had sunk his backside into the sofa. She straightened the lampshade and disappeared into the hall. Bill returned to the sports section. There wasn't much reading in it, for it was a weekday and he wasn't one for the horses or the snooker. He was just beginning to think about a cup of tea when June called out to him from the kitchen.

'I might just go out and sweep them up.'

'Sweep what up, Love?'

'The leaves, on the front doorstep, and yon dirty great Twix wrapper. It's disgusting. I don't want it to be the first thing our Maureen sees when she arrives.'

'It's the East we live in, June, not bloody Cherry Valley. The rubbish on our doorstep'll not be the first disgusting thing your sister sees this afternoon. There's a whole world of dog shit waiting for her to plough through, not to mention the broken bottles and what them wee hallions wrote across the chip-shop shutters the other night.'

June didn't answer. He thought she might not have heard, or perhaps he'd gone too far in trying to be the funny man. The East had always sat between them like a Christmas tree left too long into the new year. Bill loved it. He was a Cregagh man born and bred. He drank in a bar with no windows and had, until his retirement, worked the line at Short's and bought his Friday-night fish supper from the Bethany. The East ran through him like blood or piss, and though he'd always promised June that someday they'd buy a place in Holywood or Ards, as close to Bangor as they could afford, he'd never had any intention of leaving the Cregagh Road. June tolerated the East because she loved him and because the human temperament will eventually grow accustomed to anything short of strangulation. However, he knew the sound of the people grated on her. The dirt of it was beneath her polished upbringing and the little streets, with their houses leaning one against the next like packed bookshelves, made her feel claustrophobic. (They made Bill feel safe, as he had once felt close and safe, tucked between his two older brothers in the ancient bed they'd shared as children.)

June was still in the kitchen, hoaking through the cleaning cupboard for a yard brush. The front of her had disappeared into the clutter of stepladders and mop buckets. All Bill could see was her backside twitching in its tweedy skirt. She was not wearing her 'going out' pants and he could see the line where her knickers were cutting into the flesh of her hips. He felt sorry for her and also a little disgusted, which immediately made him feel angry with himself and anxious to make amends.

'Uch, I'm sorry, pet,' he said, patting her lightly on the rump.

At his touch June unbent suddenly. Her head, still consumed

by the cleaning cupboard made sharp contact with a shelf and there was a peel of metallic nips and clicks as tins and bottles tumbled to the ground.

'Shit,' she said.

June was not by nature a religious woman, yet rarely swore. The sound of the word, muffled as it was by mops, dusters and various cleaning rags, was a little desperate, a little like a bird, trapped in a room with no door. Bill hauled his wife out of the cupboard by her belt. She was crying when he turned her round.

'Sorry,' she said.

She was still holding the wad of cotton wool in one hand, filthy with the dust from the blinds. Bill thought she might use it to wipe her eyes and so he reached for a tissue from the box on top of the microwave.

'No, June,' he said firmly. 'I'm the one who should be sorry. I shouldn't have been winding you up like that. Sure, amn't I the lucky man to have a wife who keeps the place so nice. Your woman next door lets her fella live in a pigsty and here's you treating me like the king of East Belfast for the last forty years. I'm an ungrateful sod for not appreciating you more. I should buy you flowers sometimes.'

Bill manoeuvred June onto a seat and filled the kettle. Without thinking, he made her coffee in one of the mugs which had come free with an Easter egg, the sort of mug that only ever came out when the dishwasher was full. He registered her disapproval as he sat it in front of her. She managed not to pass comment. It was rare enough for Bill to make a cuppa, without critiquing his style. He put two Jammie Dodgers and a Jaffa Cake on a saucer and set it on the table beside her coffee. June didn't touch them, but she seemed pleased to see him trying.

'You take ten minutes to yourself, wee love,' Bill said, 'I'll go out and give the doorstep a bit of a lick and a promise. It's the least I can do.' He leant over and kissed his wife on the top of her head. She smelt like a brown paper bag.

'Will you do the pavement in front of the house while you're at it?' she asked.

Bill bit his tongue. The pavement outside their house had been an ongoing issue since his retirement. Bill didn't see why they should take responsibility for a bit of land which belonged to the city council. June neither agreed nor disagreed with her husband. She'd been listening to his argument for months now and scrubbing away regardless, going at the asphalt with a stiff yard brush and a basin of soapy water so the ten square feet in front of their house was now a lighter, brighter shade of black than the rest of the street. She was proud of this and did not seem to realise she was maintaining a blank canvas for every gum-dropping youth and shitting Jack Russell in a five-block radius. In the East, it didn't serve to try too hard at anything, even when it came to keeping your front step clean.

'Will you give the pavement a wee quick going over?' she repeated.

'I will,' said Bill, 'just for you. Though dear only knows why we're paying our rates when the council barely lift a finger round here.'

She shushed him like a baby, raising a finger to her lips, and nodded towards the cupboard where the yard brush lived.

'Be quick,' she said, 'our Maureen'll be here any second.'

When he turned round she'd tidied his *News Letter* off the counter and into the recycling bin. Her coffee had not been touched, but one of the Jammie Dodgers was gone.

'I'll only be a second, love,' said Bill.

He wondered if he'd have time to nip down the road for a jumbo Twix. He'd already had one that morning but it was shaping up to be a two-Twix kind of day.

'Here, Bill,' she cried out as he went to leave. He paused for a minute in the doorway between the kitchen and the hall, brush clutched in his right hand like an old-fashioned crutch. 'I meant that I'm sorry about everything. You know, the way it's changed between me and you,' she said.

'We can talk about it later, June, after your sister,' Bill snapped. It was imperative that he cut her off, before she said something too honest. 'You're just tired and wound up about Maureen. It's not a big deal. Honestly, we're grand.'

He left June sitting at the table twisting a hankie between her fingers as her coffee skinned and cooled in its creme egg mug. It *was* a big deal. They were *not* grand but he didn't know how to say this without starting a thing which could not be stopped or even slowed down. It was best to skirt around the edges of ugly situations, like that time there hadn't been a baby for years and they'd just kept trying, every other day without saying, until eventually there had been a baby and it was once again all right to say generous things such as, 'That's great news, pet,' and, 'Sure, wasn't it worth the wait.'

Bill closed the door behind him and felt in his pocket. He could tell without looking that he'd enough change for a jumbo Twix and a bottle of Lucozade but the inclination had left him. He paused for a moment on their 'Welcome' mat, resting his weight on the broom handle. A pigeon eyed him from the kerb, the black of its eye twitching like a tiny, tiny cue ball. Bill hated pigeons. In general, he was not much of a man for animals which couldn't be eaten, but he reserved his deepest loathing for birds. He found pigeons particularly provocative and, when presented with the opportunity, liked to kick them or swipe at them with blunt instruments. Bill stepped suddenly forwards now, stabbing his yard brush at the bird so it rose like smoke from a stubbed cigarette. He failed to catch even the fleeting tip of its wing.

'Damn you,' he muttered to no one in particular, and the pigeon, but most likely June, who could not hear through the front door and the second internal door separating the hall from their kitchen. The street was empty, and Bill immediately felt foolish for bringing a noise into it. He placed the bristled end of his brush on the pavement and began sweeping. His first thrust caught the Twix wrapper and several blackening leaves. He swept again and found dust, a till receipt from the off-licence, thin diamonds of green and brown glass, also ring pulls. On the third stroke he hit dirt. There was a satisfaction in seeing black asphalt bloom beneath the dust. Bill stood for a moment, admiring the sweep of his clean. It was not a new sensation. He remembered it from the time when he'd owned a car and gone at it with a chamois leather on the weekend, moving the polish up and down till the shine was evenly spread and consistent. Bill swept on and, in a matter of minutes, had formed a peaked pile of dust and litter. The table-sized square in front of their house was clean. This would please June, and this should have pleased Bill. But it didn't.

He had no idea what to do with the dust. He had not thought to lift a pan and, in the street, there was no such thing as a rug for brushing it under. Using the broom, he nudged the pile across the invisible line marking their world from the world next door. It came to rest like a sacrificial mound, soft and vaguely threatening, outside his neighbours' door. A stick had come with it and a balled up flier for the SuperValu on the corner. This did not seem fair. The people next door were not the worst by far in a street of trying individuals. So Bill swept on, deferring the mess to the next house down. The next house down was Polish: a young couple with a child and an elderly lady who wore a dress over men's slacks and might have belonged to either the girl or the fella. It didn't seem right to leave the dirt on their doorstep. The old lady might read into it some kind of insult or the young couple might feel unwelcome in their own home. It wasn't right with a child in the house either. Bill swept their pavement for them, collecting dust, more dust and an empty plastic bottle which had once contained Coke Zero. The space where his arms hinged onto his shoulders began to pool with sweat.

He looked up and thought he saw Maureen approaching from the far end of the street. The swing of her arms was particularly distinctive. He'd often thought she carried herself like one of those rural electricity pylons, striding greedily across some poor farmer's fields. She was carrying a green plastic bag from Marks and Spencer and, as she approached, Bill remembered that Maureen had always seen carrier bags as common. (Maureen's list of things perceived to be common was long and without reason, extending as it did to pre-packaged cheese slices, vending machines, Channel 4 sitcoms and ladies who wore any colour but demure red on their fingernails.) This was not his sister-in-law, but rather a lady unfortunate enough to resemble Maureen in shape and general demeanour. This was not his sister-in-law, but any minute now Maureen would appear around the corner and Bill would be obliged to open his door to her and tolerate her talking for the rest of the evening.

He leant on the broom handle, wiping the sweat from his brow with the cuff-edge of his sleeve. The job was done. He could go back into the house and finish the farming supplement, maybe even watch a bit of Sky Sports until Maureen arrived. June would be pleased. She'd make him tea in a proper mug and look at him like he'd just come back from the war. The thought of this made Bill's insides constrict. Once, a year back, he'd humoured June with ballroom dancing. She'd seen it on the television. She thought they could do it together, something new to try now he was retired. On the dance floor, in his funeral trousers and his patent shoes, Bill had felt like the sort of man who did jigsaw puzzles on the dining-room table. 'I feel like a prize wanker,' he'd said to June. She'd never mentioned the dancing again and had gone the next week with her friend Lynda from Ballybeen. Bill looked at his own front door and felt like he was swallowing a ballroom all over again. The quiet in there would kill him, and then later there would be Maureen.

'Sure, I've started now,' he muttered under his breath, 'I might as well finish the job.'

There were only five houses to the corner of their street. Bill decided to keep on sweeping. Just on their side of the road of course. He wasn't martyr enough to do the other side. He would do this for June, he told himself, make the place look nice so she wouldn't be mortified when her sister arrived. It was good when you wanted to do something for yourself and there was an excuse which fit it exactly, making it seem like the right thing to do.

Sure, amn't I the good husband, Bill was telling himself as he reached the end of their street. He felt the urge to keep sweeping all the way up the Cregagh and onwards in the direction of Dundonald. He didn't even try to stop himself. The pile of dirt was bigger than a handbag now. There was a dead bird in it and a used condom. He tried not to look at either item directly. He tried not to think about things coming apart, spilling into each other like bread and gristle mixing in the compost bin.

At five he stopped outside a wee Tesco. It was almost three hours since he'd started sweeping and he was hungry. He leant his yard brush against the window and went in for a jumbo Twix and a bottle of Lucozade. The Lucozade was cool in the bottle and bubbling like fish breath. Bill held it in front of his face. He could see it and also through it. The liquid inside the bottle was almost the same colour as the sky setting over East Belfast. This struck him as beautiful, like on a postcard. He was not normally a romantic man and did not know where to put this thought. It swelled in him like heartburn or the bloating pride he'd come to associate with pipe bands and Van Morrison and the shipyard cranes, striding across the East Belfast skyline like bow-legged bandits from another place.

'It's not such a bad wee bit of the world is it?' he said to the next person he passed. This person did not speak to him or even acknowledge Bill's presence, for Bill was an elderly man in his shirtsleeves, and it was almost dark and he was still sweeping. A thumbprint of chocolate had smudged itself into the flesh between his chin and his mouth. June would not have tolerated this. June would have gone at it with a damp cloth, but June was not here. Bill tried to picture her in the kitchen with Maureen, wondering when he might come home.

'It's not like Bill,' she was saying and her hands were cradled around a cooling tea cup.

And Maureen was not saying anything, though they both knew she wanted to.

Bill looked at the yard brush. It felt good in his hands. He wondered if other men might feel the same way about guns. *I could do another hour*, he thought, *if the light holds*. It was a pleasant evening and could still be considered summer. There was nothing in particular stopping Bill. There was more than enough dirt in East Belfast to keep him from June for as long as he wished.

10.

Floater

Your father was an open door. Your mother, a thumb-nosed fool. And you, for your sins – insignificant though they may be – were conceived in an airplane bathroom.

Don't get the wrong idea, kiddo. It was a pleasant-enough bathroom, generously proportioned and fitted with not one but two conveniently located life vests. There was a small sink, barely large enough to squeeze both hands beneath the tap, and, mounted on the back of this sink, two dispensers: the first for soap and the second for hand lotion. Both smelt soundly of pear drops. The paper towels descended in frisky cotton wads from beneath the mirror. The bin was a trapdoor. The toilet, when it flushed, was furious, suckering every last teaspoonful of excrement into outer space as if determined to sever all association with freshly laid shit. The door folded in upon itself, like the wings of a paper airplane pinching in anticipation of flight. When closed, there was barely enough space for two full-grown adults to stand. Your father was forced to sit on me as he manoeuvred himself out the door. We were strangers again, and his trousered buttocks advancing towards my groin seemed an oddly, intimate epitaph.

Everything was neat, everything was useful; your father and I were the only deviations in an otherwise faultless space. I'd have preferred a hotel.

At the point of your conception I was a nineteen-year-old girl with average-sized feet. I say 'average', though in all honesty 'generous', or even 'enormous', might be more fitting descriptions.

I was very well grounded. I can only assume your father to have been similarly blessed.

Your father's feet, as I last remember them, backing through the bathroom door, were of average length and breadth for a middle-aged man. Save for the normal squirming and repositioning, the sort of behaviour to be expected given the cramped conditions, all our feet remained reassuringly attached to the bathroom floor for the duration of our encounter.

Your father said many wise and witty things, none of which broke air in my presence.

'Goodness,' your father once said (the only thing I can clearly remember), 'this soap reeks of something I can't quite place.'

'Pear drops,' I mumbled, bent double, arranging the tails of my skirt. But your father had already unfolded the door.

Surely we should not blame the airplane bathroom for everything that followed.

★

I keep you anchored to the backyard fence by a single piece of purple ribbon. It crucifies me on a daily basis.

I am scared to give you more than fifteen feet. After fifteen feet, it looks like you are disappearing. Your head begins to scrape the lower clouds. Your hands are doll's hands. Your feet shrink to two small commas, caught up in a pair of ballet pumps. I can see right up your skirt. I should buy you tracksuit bottoms.

After fifteen feet, you no longer seem like yourself. We can't even have a proper conversation without yelling.

'Mama!' you shout, cupping both hands to form a question mark. 'Can I come down yet?'

In the kitchen, where I am washing the breakfast dishes, I can see the lower half of your heels dangling in the window: red shoes today, with black, block heels. I can barely hear you over the dishes.

'What's that you say, sweetheart?' I ask, walking outside with the dishcloth still damp in my hands.

You repeat the question (more loudly this time for the benefit of our neighbours, who are judgmental to the right of our fence, and nosy as sin to the left). 'Mama, can I come down yet?'

You've been asking the same question every morning for the past four years. I have yet to arrive at a satisfactory answer.

At first you could not manage words. You spoke spit and tantrums, heavy sentiments which fell into my flowerbeds, suffocating all but the hardiest perennials. Now you simply ask. You are polite, respectful and, lately, hesitant, as if finally coming to terms with a life spent floating fifteen feet off the ground.

You have come to understand the importance of restraint. You smile constantly, though from down here, no one can see your teeth.

'Mama,' you ask on the hour, every hour since I bought you that digital watch last Christmas, 'can I come down yet?'

'Not just yet, sweetheart,' I holler from the back patio.

'But there's nothing to do up here. There's no one to talk to.'

I find myself catching the tears in a wad of kitchen roll as I remind you of birds and flying insects and the ever-present possibility of a passing hot-air balloon. 'God's probably up there somewhere,' I add. 'He loves it when you talk to him.'

I can hear you smiling all the way down the ribbon. You've

trained yourself to keep smiling. You're a clever kid. You already know how the world works. Social Services will take you away if, for even a second, you look like you aren't enjoying the view.

Social Services are a constant drag. Having nothing to measure me against, they use hitters and kickers and people who do ruinous things to small children. They throw questions like answers and seem to think you'd fare better with a different mother. 'It's not normal,' they say, eyebrows arching over their plastic-backed clipboards. Yet they cannot find an official excuse to remove you. They say I am a distant mother. They say we need to spend more time together, with other people, in other places, and I say it's not for lack of trying. Social Services visit once a week, twice if one of the neighbours has reported us again.

The neighbours are abysmal.

The church folk are even worse.

They are 'concerned', approaching our doorstep under cover of holy prayer and casserole. They are just as nosy as the unconcerned people who peer through our living-room window, hoping for a good dinner party anecdote. They take notes on your dervish hair, the bruise where the ribbon bites your ankle, and your skirt, which is more often than not circling your shoulders like a Superman cape. They are very much concerned. They return with further casseroles and tracksuit bottoms, as if we could not afford to buy our own. When I say, 'No thank you, I'd prefer if you didn't pray in my living room,' they say, 'Fine,' and 'No problem,' and, 'Can I get my casserole dish back when you're finished with it?' Their concern curdles quicker than left-out milk.

The last thing we need is a room full of concerned strangers. Our situation is complicated in a way strangers can never quite comprehend. 'All she needs is a pair of scissors,' they say, fishing through their handbags for a quick solution. 'That child needs bringing down to earth right this instant.'

It's not like we haven't tried scissors. It's not like we haven't tried magnets and lead weights, Velcro shoes and anchors. Nothing works. It is impossible to keep you down.

It bears repeating kiddo; the last thing we need is a room full of strangers armed with nail scissors and good intentions.

'Mama,' you say, barely audible now, 'why do I have to stay here?'

And, though I have no good answer, no answer at all, I still smile and shout, 'It's only for a little while longer, sweetheart. Just a little while longer.'

★

Your father wore a suit jacket for the duration of our encounter. If I'm entirely honest, I noticed the suit jacket long before I noticed your father, sweating inside it. Your father had a face like a blunt doorknob. I did not find him attractive at first. I did not find him attractive after the event, but something about the suit jacket caught kindly at the back of my throat.

I offered him a stick of gum. He accepted. We were old acquaintances by this stage, fifteen minutes at least: exactly the time it takes for an average-sized commercial airplane to trundle down the runway, take off and tuck its wheels, like retiring genitals, back inside its undercarriage.

I'd chosen my seat for its proximity to the emergency exit. In those days, I still feared an ill-defined worst. Your father slipped into the seat once removed from mine just minutes before departure and, while I have always preferred an empty row, something about his presence made my lungs feel looser. As the wheels left the ground I glanced to my right, past the empty seat and the airplane magazines, and straight into your father's open face. I read a benediction in the furrowed lines stitching his right eyebrow to his left. All previous plans flew out the window.

Somewhere above the Isle of Man, our fingers fought loose, hovering over the empty seat belt until eventually they found each other and locked soundly. For thirty-five minutes, we were incendiary, your father and I, like two young things tottering on the edge of unbelief. I commented on his reading material: the French writer, not the obvious one. He complimented my hair, my eyes, my legs and – twenty minutes later, with the back of my head reflected in the bathroom mirror – the diamond-shaped cluster of freckles at the base of my neck.

You're old enough to know it wasn't love or even alcohol. I have wondered, over the years, about the altitude, the in-flight peanuts, the piped airline music, hardly the best preamble to romance. I have blamed the suit jacket and the way your father clasped my hand deliberately, our fingers forming a cantilever bridge across the empty seat. I have reached no satisfactory conclusion, and can only claim, for justification, the sensation of hovering beyond gravity's pinch, suspended between one world of ordinary and the next. Stranger things have happened in the empty space between up and down.

God only knows how we found our way to the bathroom. The soap dispenser had more sense than your father and I combined.

He said the knee socks, puddling drunkenly around my ankles, made him feel like a teenager again.

He said I was good-looking for a bigger girl.

He said my feet reminded him of shipyard barges, and stood lightly on the tips of my shoes, flattening the space where my toes ran out. 'No chance of you floating away, love,' he said, and I could not tell if he meant this as a compliment or not.

He said, 'I'm old enough to be your da,' and I expect he was, and this realisation neither thrilled nor turned me. Perhaps I am to blame for everything that followed.

In the bathroom, by the soap dispenser, with the smell of pear drops sickly in my throat, I was little more than a notion of myself. I watched my face, profiled in the mirror. I could see the back of your father's head going at me like a blunt instrument. He was balding at the back, his hair parted to reveal a sausage-pink swirl exactly the shape and size of a fried egg. I wondered what other calamities I might be capable of.

About twenty seconds before you fizzled onto the scene, your father offered me his name – both names – formally, accompanied by a handshake of sorts. By this stage, it was too late to stop you. A familiar fist clenched in the pit of my belly. The plane lurched under us as if nodding consent, and when your father finally slid free, fastening his suit jacket sharply, I found myself fat with the knowledge of you: a coy and furious creature, pounding your presence like a caged burp.

'Hey,' I said, 'what sort of thing did you leave inside me?' but your father had already found the door handle.

I sat on the toilet lid, pulled both knees to my chin and cried one moderate tear, bell-shaped like an old-fashioned pear drop. Denouncing gravity, the tear floated up to meet the ceiling.

I lingered on the airplane toilet for the rest of the flight. No one seemed to notice my empty seat. When the wheels hit the runway, I glanced upwards, only to find that the small circle of tear water had vanished. The sad certainty of you had already burrowed through the ceiling, through the walls and wires of the airplane and ever upwards, keeping faith with the water cycle.

Even then, exactly thirteen minutes thicker with the love of you, I knew that nothing would be ordinary again.

★

When it rains, as it often does in our street, I reel you in, one foot of florist's ribbon at a time. I keep you in the attic. In the centre section, where the house is highly pitched, you can get a good six feet of air. It's barely sufficient, but better than the cloakroom closet.

Your head scrapes constantly against the ceiling, so I've stapled pillows across the rafters. Even so, winters are hard. The hair begins to wear thin on the crown of your head. Your elbows throb for the open sky. Your head aches from lack of elevation. At night, in your sleep, smile firmly fixed, you hum love songs to the higher clouds, the thin places which coast above the rain. Perhaps you think I can't hear, but the walls in this house are exceptionally thin.

I love you.

I tell you this. 'I love you,' I say, speaking firmly over the hissing water, each and every time I wrestle you under the showerhead. It takes both arms and a safety harness to hold you down. 'I love you,' I say and kiss the space where you should be: eating breakfast at the kitchen table like a normal six-year-old, tucked under the blankets which cannot keep you down, hanging from the monkey bars in the People's Park. 'I love you,' I say, tugging on the end of your purple ribbon to make a point, 'but I'm not quite sure how to make this work.'

'Don't worry, Mama,' you shout, turning upside down to look me in the eye, 'I'm going to pray that God gives you wings so you can come up here too.'

I would like to agree, to scream 'Amen!' at the top of my twenty-six-year-old lungs and join you somewhere above the telephone wires, but I have to be honest. On days like today, when my legs look longer than even yesterday, and the attractive postman has grown his beard out, and I, for all my backyard problems, do not feel a day over twenty-three – on most days, if I'm absolutely honest – I want to forget about the little girl tied to my garden fence.

'Surely,' I think to myself, 'God cannot still be upset about
the airplane bathroom.'

★

You were not like other unborns. You did not sleep. You twitched
constantly, like a trapped sneeze.

Fists up from the very first second, you were grazing the roof
of my belly for a skylight. After twenty weeks, the outlines of
your tiny hands – already poised for flight – appeared like second
and third belly buttons, just above my belt.

I was ashamed, on account of the airplane bathroom and
your father, the only open door on our street. I wore a potato
sack and told no one, until finally the potato sack could no longer
hide the cut of your wrists and elbows, protruding through my
stretch marks.

'Good Lord,' the lady at the hospital said, holding to the light
your ultrasound slides, 'it looks like you're giving birth to Superman . . . or Supergirl,' she quickly corrected herself, the space
between your legs still a mystery to me.

'Should I be worried?' I asked, propping myself up for a better view. 'It doesn't feel like a baby. It feels more like a balloon.
Could it possibly be the airplane bathroom?'

'Stuff and nonsense. You can't go blaming airplane bathrooms. It's probably just indigestion or the way you slept last
night. Get some rest. Place a sandbag on your belly. Everything
will be just fine.'

Things were far from textbook. You swelled daily, inflating
with every breath I took. By the third trimester I was one part
baby and six parts space. The doctor had nothing new to say. I
asked for a second opinion and this doctor was equally dumb-
struck. 'I'll look it up on the Internet,' she said. I could just as
easily have done this at home.

I was unsure where you'd belong in a world so taken with gravity.

At the local swimming pool – enormous now, a double-decker bus swathed in a floral bathing suit – I tried to drown you. Down at the diving end, where it's nine feet deep and difficult to see, I pinched my nose and sank. It did not work. The air in you was much, much larger than me. You rose. I, reluctantly wrapped around you, also rose belly first to meet the water's surface. When the point of my chin pierced the pool's skin I opened my mouth and howled to the overhead lights for all the stupid things I had lately done in airplane bathrooms and other, more obvious rooms.

In the very last week, full term now and more than ready to deflate, I could no longer keep my feet on the ground. At night I bound myself with ribbons and belts to the foot of the bed and still woke to a good half-foot of air between the mattress and my back. Thick with shame I could not even tell the midwife, and next evening tied the knots tighter, hoping to delay your very first flight.

'God,' I prayed, to the curtains and the duvet cover, but most of all the carpet, which remained reassuringly underfoot, 'do not let me be a single day overdue. Not a single day, you hear me. I don't want this special thing inside me one minute longer than necessary.' And just like that, Jesus wept, my waters broke and you came floating out to meet the world, six pounds thick and lighter than air.

If it wasn't for the cord – a good invention on God's part – I might have lost you instantly.

★

This morning I wake to find the scissors already waiting.

'It isn't cruel. It's for the best,' I tell myself. 'It's the most natural thing in the world.'

I take a long shower. I wash my hair twice. I fix breakfast and float it up to you attached to a helium-filled balloon. I don't, for a second, let the scissors out of my sight.

I watch an episode of *Murder, She Wrote*. The scissors are winking at me from the coffee table by the window. 'Snip,' they say, 'Snip, snip, snip and then tomorrow morning the postman, the girls for coffee, part-time jobs and cruise ships – no strings attached.'

'Snip, snip, snip.' They make it sound so easy.

I fix pancakes for your lunch, pancakes and chocolate-chip ice cream. 'What's wrong, Mama?' you shout down to me (you are more than accustomed to your five portions of fruit and veg daily). 'Is it my birthday again?'

'No, sweetheart,' I say, fingering the scissors in my apron pocket. 'We're having ice cream for lunch because I love you.'

'Oh. Can I come down now?'

I feel terrible. I try to trip over your ribbon, hoping it might be an accident. I tug vigorously on the blessed thing but it simply won't snap. Finally, I resort to the scissors. It is remarkably easy to let you go.

At first nothing changes. Your feet hover momentarily fifteen feet above the azaleas. I focus on the bottoms of your sneakers, which from this distance are white blobs, roughly the size and shape of two aspirin tablets. The remains of the purple ribbon wrap round the garden fence and prepare to weather the next ten years alone. The ice-cream dish drops suddenly, falling to earth with a clumsy thud. Then, as if gravity has finally given up, the sky sucks you home.

You are a six-year-old girl. You are an oversized doll. You are a bird, a balloon and finally a small, red fleck on the afternoon sky.

I strain my eyes for the very last seconds of you, running inside for the binoculars.

There is a lightness inside me now, a warm spacious feeling, like a greenhouse but colder. Most likely, by the time you hit the sky's ceiling, instantly turning to clouds and rain, I will have forgotten you. By the time you pass God and go racing after the planets I will have myself a brand new baby with ordinary feet.

I expect you understand – you've always been a very understanding little girl – but if, in the instant before evaporation, your very last thought is anger, do not blame me. Do not blame yourself. Blame the airplane bathroom and your father, who was only there for the easy part.

11.

How They Were Sitting When Their Wings Fell Off

When they returned from the hospital there was a bouquet of flowers on the doorstep. It was unusually warm for September. The heat had caused the chrysanthemums to wilt so they leant against the door like elderly men folding over their walking sticks. 'From the Wilsons, with deepest sympathy,' Steven read, without fully understanding, and slipped the card into his back pocket. He opened the door with one hand and helped his wife into the apartment. Leaving her on the living-room couch, he returned for her overnight bag and returned again to gaze up and down the corridor, convinced they'd left something behind. Closing the door behind him, he forgot all about the flowers.

The lights inside the apartment were just as loud as they'd left them. There had not been time to consider the lights or other practicalities such as the cat, the central heating or even coats. 'Now,' his wife had said, 'we need to go now.' She'd been in the bathroom, and he, installed as was his usual custom, in the kitchen fixing dinner. He'd caught her face reflected in the glass sheen of the microwave door and, turning with a casserole dish in hand, knew that it was already too late. She had not been crying then. Neither had she cried on the way to the hospital, but she'd held his hand like an emergency exit, all nails and tight urgency. She'd left her mark on Steven's wrist: four half-moon crescents and a single penny-sized bruise where her thumb had pressed into his pulse. Thus attached, it was almost impossible to change gears, but he'd managed, dragging her hand sharply this way and that as they navigated the town's roundabouts and stoplights.

He'd parked outside the hospital in the spot reserved for ambulances. In ordinary circumstances Steven was the sort of man who could not break rules, who returned library books two days early and grew anxious eating shop-bought snacks in the cinema. Yet some sharper authority had seized him today and he'd understood himself capable of theft and violence and loud, loud shouting, should the need arise. 'Let me,' he said as his wife struggled to remove the seatbelt and lever her mountainous belly out of the car. He'd wondered then if he had the audacity to carry her, like an old-fashioned hero, across the parking lot and into the hospital's foyer. She was heavier now than he was, and it would have been a tremendous struggle. But, in the moment, he'd understood that it was not practicality which bound him so much as propriety and the fear of drawing attention to himself.

Once his wife had eased herself out of the car and stood, bracing her weight against its open door, Steven noticed that a dark pool had crept out of her, covering the passenger seat like a lost continent. Leaning into the car, he drew the stench of her into his lungs: rust, brine and the shrill pinch of ammonia. This was a language his wife had never spoken before. He closed the door upon it quickly. All that wetness, the sensation of being emptied in waves: surely she must have known, and yet she hadn't cried out, had only sunk her fingernails further into his wrist and said, over and over, her words keeping time with the fleeting streetlamps, 'It'll be all right, Steven. It will be all right.' Locking the car, he'd turned her face towards the hospital door, blocked her from behind, made sure she could not look back. 'It'll be all right,' he said. And everything would be all right if only they could look down the side of their sadness, keep themselves from staring at it directly, like roadkill, or war on the television news.

In the rush, Steven hadn't thought to turn the lights off and, hours later, sitting on a chair outside the operating theatre, would wonder if he'd even locked the apartment door. It was strange what the human mind could fixate upon in a crisis. Once, in the A & E at Antrim Area Hospital, he'd sat opposite a man who'd cut his own arm off with a chainsaw, accidentally whilst trimming the hedges. It was possible, the man explained, that the arm could still be reattached. It sat next to his feet in a picnic cooler packed full of frozen peas and potato waffles. The man kept his good hand resting like a guard dog on the lid of the cooler, his missing hand bandaged and elevated above his head. Every few minutes or so, as if all this, even the blood, was no more remarkable than a long bath, he'd stopped a passing nurse or doctor to enquire after the evening's football results.

It was strange what the human mind would fixate upon in a crisis. There was a poster pinned to the wall outside the operating theatre: 'Breast is best for your child.' Steven had read every word on this poster, even the phone numbers. He made anagrams from the longer words, all the time wondering why his mind could not catch on the thought of his wife's belly, split and peeled back like an open-mouthed whale. There would be blood and machines, he reminded himself, various cutting knives. Afterwards there would be a child and there would also be the space left behind a child. Yet, these truths were not in the moment as believable as the poster in front of him or the uncomfortable plastic chair driving its mean ridges into the undersides of his thighs.

The doctor had told him everything in the corridor, standing up, shaking hands so their arms met in the middle like rafters, or two men holding each other at a terrible distance. At the far end of the corridor a porter appeared pushing an older man slowly towards them in a wheelchair. Though Steven could not explain the urgency, it felt imperative that they finish their conversation and part before the porter could draw close enough to overhear. He'd tightened his grip on the doctor's hand, leant in as if intending to kiss or bring his forehead suddenly down upon the other man's nose. A coffee stain, no bigger than a common grape, was blooming across the lapel of the doctor's coat. Steven could smell the caffeine still furring on his breath and pictured him downing his espresso neat in the staff canteen, settling his nerves for this very moment. 'Thank you,' he'd said, his hand still cuffing the doctor's, and wondered exactly what he was thankful for. He was older than this doctor, as was his wife.

Five minutes later, the nurse had also told him everything in the relatives' room, sitting down with sweet tea and a saucer full of biscuits. He counted the biscuits for something to focus upon: three rich teas and a pair of Bourbon creams, rectangling over the saucer's edge like trouser legs, kicking. 'I don't take sugar in my tea,' he said sharply, and she blushed, apologised and scurried off to replace his cup with something more bitter. *Sweet tea for the shock*, he'd thought. He knew this from books and also movies, but the very thought of it was bile in his mouth. He should have apologised to the nurse. None of the hospital had been her fault, even the tea. And yet, when she'd returned with a mug and a separate jug of milk, he'd been overcome by the desire to spit in her smiling, smiling face and it was all he could manage to take the mug and hold it between his hands until, at last, it grew too cold to drink.

In the end it had not been like television and in the end it had been just like television. All those on-screen losses, both British and American, and very occasionally foreign, had prepared him well. He'd known what to say, when to stand, how to hold his hands like an absent father. He'd felt himself folding along familiar lines: an actor catching his own shadow on an advertisement for toothpaste or expensive yogurt. 'Can I see my wife now?' he asked. Under the circumstances, he would be expected to see her. He had not wanted to see her. Without the baby she would not look the same. And she would see herself different in the way he looked at her and later held her, like an egg already fractured.

There was nothing to say on the way back from the hospital. They were no more or less than they had been on the previous day, but the car seemed to be struggling to contain them and he'd rolled down the window on both sides, hoping this would give their sadness room enough to breathe. His wife began crying before they left the car park, turning away from him so he could only see her tears in profile. She had not bothered to reach for his hand or even ask for a tissue. Drawing the sun visor down to check her make-up, she'd caught sight of the child's car seat, marooned as it now was, in the back seat. 'Sorry,' he'd said, and even this, the simplest of sentiments, had sounded exactly like a shotgun emptying into a quiet room.

It had been Steven's job to deal with the details, and here he was stumbling at the first, small funeral. At the next set of traffic lights he stopped, unhooked the seat and left it leaning against a lamppost. It would remain there for a week, apologising for itself every time he drove to the garage or the twenty-four-hour Tesco at the end of their road. He would have liked to have burnt it –

watched the polyester lining blacken and curl into itself like unconfessed sin – but it would be months before he had the stomach for such blasphemy.

'It's gone now, love,' he'd said as he returned to their car. He meant the car seat, but could not be sure that she'd understood him correctly.

The apartment was just where they'd left it, in a west-side apartment block, cut and coloured the unremarkable shade of corrugated card. It was still bordered, to the left and right, by similar apartments. Their neighbours were young couples, recently married or cohabitating. Many, if not all, kept dogs: smaller, indoor breeds which would, when the time arrived, do well with babies and children. Their neighbours had 'Welcome' mats outside their doors, holly wreaths at Christmas and occasionally a pumpkin for Halloween. They were, in this and other crucial aspects, as close to American as Belfast would permit. Several of their neighbours were also called Steven, though most, when in the company of friends or work colleagues, preferred Steve.

More than half had opted for black patent doors. 'Classy,' they said, when asked why they'd chosen this colour over the more traditional browns, greens and fireman-reds. 'Postmodern, urban, industrial.' Sometimes, late at night, when he had the strong drink on him, Steven would misplace his own apartment in this sea of shallow steps and identical front doors. He would only realise his mistake when the key refused to turn and the mirrored black of his neighbour's door revealed him fumbling at the lock like a first-time lover.

Their apartment was not as he'd remembered it from a distance. Parking his car on the street outside their door, Steven stared at his own home. He noted the windows, the security light and, mounted on the wall next to the door, the aluminium plate which housed all twenty-six apartments' buzzers. Someone on the first floor had filled a planter with late-flowering nasturtiums and placed it on their windowsill. The flaming yellows and oranges roared at him like tiny, trumpet-faced lions. He allowed his eye to drift upwards and, on the third floor next to the spouting, found the square interruption of their bathroom window, the faint outline of shampoo bottles and shower gels ghosting behind its frosted glass.

This was their home. They had only ever lived here together, and while there were other houses in his past – squalid, student flats off the Lisburn Road and the three generous bungalows which housed all his childhood memories – this was the only place he'd ever felt permanent. However, their apartment was not as Steven had remembered it all night, on a hospital chair, when the taste of his own bed and bathroom sink had risen to taunt him like breakfast hunger. The difference was not in the detail, but something more elemental – distance perhaps, or maybe perspective.

'We're home,' he said to his wife, and it did not feel like home. He viewed the apartment through the car's windscreen as a grown man might view a hotel or foreign guest house frequented during childhood. There the trees; there the steps they'd once sat upon eating ice cream; there the postbox and the place where she'd tripped and, in falling, scattered the weekend's groceries across the pavement, muddling eggs and orange juice, milk and ketchup like a spilt sunset. All was familiar and at the same time faded, as if the previous day's events had drawn the colour out of their memories. He could no longer be certain that they'd ever been happy here.

Steven helped her out of the car.

'Can you manage the stairs?' he asked, and his wife dipped her chin and raised it once, a gesture as slight and remarkable as the optimistic incline on a French 'e'.

They took the stairs gently, placing both feet on each step before progressing to the next. She was still wearing the slippers they'd loaned her at the hospital, and her feet slipped backwards and forwards like loose fish. She wore his left arm as a belt, pitching her weight against his ribcage. Each careful step threw them up against each other and they were two blind things colliding in a darkened room. Though it was no time for pride or anything so upright, Steven was proud of her and also proud of himself, the pride increasing as they ascended towards the first floor, the second and, finally, the third. All along their corridor he prayed that the neighbours would keep their doors shut, and they did. He counted the doors down in colours rather than numbers – black, black, green – and on the third black, arrived at his own door with the chrysanthemums.

The apartment still smelt like their apartment. They had only been absent for forty-eight hours. The curtains remained drawn in every curtained room. The table was still set for dinner. Their everyday plates circled the cutlery and condiments like disappointed satellites, awaiting a meal which would never make the four-foot journey from oven to dining table. In the centre of the table, the salad had shrivelled into itself. The bread, on the breadboard, had crusted, and the Parmesan had returned to oil and milky whey. Only the individual waters, clear and impartial in their half-pint glasses, remained unaffected by the previous day's events.

Steven dropped his keys instinctively on the telephone table. Falling, they made the sound of coins settling. He chose to ignore the urgent, red light pulsing on their answering machine. Later he would press the delete button, but in the first instance even this small gesture felt too deliberate, too much like a certainty. He went to hang his coat up in the cloakroom and remembered he was not wearing a coat and had not changed his pullover or jeans in almost two days. He thought about taking a shower and this was enough to provoke a hunger in him for ordinary things such as freshly brushed teeth and sleep and toast with butter and jam. *Perhaps*, he thought, *my wife might be hungry in all the same ways.*

'Cup of tea, pet?' he shouted into the living room, but his wife did not hear him or perhaps did not want tea or have the energy to answer him with actual speaking words. He would make tea anyway, present it to her on a tray with toast and hope this was not too much to ask of her, or too soon.

He slipped his shoes off and left them by the doormat. All the carpets in their apartment were the sand-blond colour of shortbread biscuits, and though they did not expect guests to remove their outdoor shoes, they had always been careful to do so themselves, preferring sock soles to slippers, and finding bare feet best of all. 'You'll not keep those clean for long when the baby arrives,' her mother had said. And she had meant the carpets and also the Chesterfield suite, which was cream, and the towels, which were white, and even their curtains, which trailed along the skirting boards like ghost tails, gathering the dust. Steven stared down at his socked toes and the carpet puckering beneath his weight and wondered if things might have been different with a blue carpet. Perhaps they had not wanted a baby enough. They were selfish people, unwilling to place their pale, uncluttered lives on the block. A dozen or more beige and oatmeal scatter cushions rose before him now, testament to the fact that they could not, or would not, compromise.

The post had piled up on the doormat next to his feet. He nudged it with the toe of his sock so the individual envelopes separated and slid across the carpet like a deck of cards, clumsily split. Their postman seemed unaware that today was not subject to the same rules as an ordinary Saturday. He'd forced the usual handful of bills and promotional fliers through their letter box.

Steven stood on the edge of the pile, considering discount coupons for the Chinese takeaway and an advertisement for Gospel meetings at the local leisure centre. There was also an electricity bill and what appeared to be a wedding invitation. It was impossible to believe in any of these so he lifted them from the mat and, balling them into a glossy, paper fist, dropped them into the recycling bin.

In the kitchen he filled the kettle and placed four slices of white bread in the toaster. The bread was too tall and even with the lever depressed fully, the slices peeked out of the individual slots: round crusts lined up, one behind the other, like marble headstones. He found two mugs unused in the cupboard and a single knife in the drawer. He placed them, with a pair of side plates, on a tray they'd been given as a wedding present. The milk had gone off but his wife often drank her tea black and he could manage without milk for once. The butter was still on the table from two evenings ago. A soap-sized remnant remained, still discernible as butter. The rest, subjected to the central heating's demands, had returned to oil and now swam around the butter dish like last night's piss lingering in the toilet bowl. He lifted the dish and tipped it into the kitchen bin and, having instigated an eviction, found himself progressing around the table as he pitched everything into the rubbish: plates, water glasses, salt and pepper, green salad weeping at the bottom of the salad bowl, bread, breadboard, lasagne, soldered as it now was to the casserole dish, cutlery and, when the table was finally bereft of even the most inconsequential item, the red gingham cloth which had previously held all their meals together.

There was little logic to Steven's actions. Tomorrow he would be faced with the choice between purchasing replacements for these lost items or fishing through the rubbish bin to retrieve them. They would not last long without cutlery. There were only so many meals which could be eaten from their hands like wolfish dogs. For the moment, however, it felt good to throw everything out, to acknowledge, in condiments and broken glassware, that nothing was permanent or worth leaning upon. Without so much as a second thought, he binned the contents of their cutlery drawer and then the spice rack, stopping just short of the larder, for he knew he should not offer his wife any excuse to starve.

He was just deliberating between a frying pan and the good corkscrew when the toaster reached the end of its cycle and spat all four slices of bread high into the air. He pinched them out of the toaster with fickle, dancing fingers and laid them across the countertop. There was no butter now, and they were not the sort of people who kept margarine, so he fixed two slices with peanut butter and a second pair spread thickly with his mother's strawberry freezer jam. Triangling them with a cheese knife, he split all four slices between the two side plates, wet the tea and carried the tray carefully into the living room.

'Tea,' he said, announcing his entrance, 'and a wee slice of toast.'

A wall had descended between Steven and his wife, and though he had, over the last five years, entered and exited this same room several thousand times unannounced, he understood that this evening and for many evenings to come it would be necessary to beg permission every time he approached her.

His wife was not on the couch where he'd left her. Neither was she sitting on the comfortable chair by the bookcase where she often sat at this hour, watching the work-day people return from their offices with laptop cases and lunch bags, long since defeated. Her hospital slippers had been arranged neatly, like two commas coupling underneath the coffee table, and her sweater lay open-armed across the footstool.

From where he stood, tray in hand, Steven could see through

the open door to their bedroom and the en-suite bathroom beyond. Both were empty. His first and most obvious fear was the nursery, but he had not left the kitchen for at least five minutes and it was impossible to arrive at the baby's room without first passing through the kitchen and dining area. It was a small apartment, awkwardly arranged and never intended for the safe housing of children. Just two weeks earlier, the box room – barely six feet square, and advertised, somewhat fraudulently, as an office space – had been hastily converted into a nursery. The baby was to have slept there in a flat-pack cot Steven had yet to remove from its packaging.

Tomorrow he would get up early and drive around town until he found a skip capable of accommodating the cot, and he would buy white paint from Homebase and cover over the pink, pink walls. He would shove each individual teddy bear to the bottom of the wheelie bin, cover their plush faces with vegetable scraps and newspapers, do everything he could to keep his wife from coming across her loss unexpectedly in a cupboard or corner.

Steven set the tray on the coffee table and went to check the cloakroom, for this was the only other place his wife might be. She was not in the cloakroom. He had not really expected to find her there amongst the coats and outdoor boots. It was a tiny closet, barely big enough to contain his golf clubs and funeral umbrella, and his wife always became anxious when presented with an enclosed space. As he opened the door and leant into the pillowy darkness, the smell of old rain and perfume fell upon him like a blanket fog. The comfort of it dragged on him with lines and tiny anchors until he found himself uncomfortable in the empty hall. He stepped into the closet, parted their various coats and, once tucked inside, drew all the coats around himself like curtains or a medieval cloak.

Just for a second, he told himself, and felt his lungs unfastening for the first time in two days.

Fumbling through the blackness, his hand found the pocket of an anorak. In the dark it was impossible to tell whether it belonged to him or his wife. He slipped his fingers inside the pocket, skirted the edges of a crumpled tissue and, nestling in the crease where one piece of fabric met another, found a single key and two copper pennies. Forced together, in the palm of his hand, they made a noise like sugar spoons colliding.

Steven drew his hand back, shocked by the sensation of cold metal in a padded place. Instinctively he raised the hand towards his face. It smelt of rust and wet October mornings; damp leaves clogging up the drains outside his office. He rubbed his hand against the thighs of his jeans, hoping to wipe away the stench and wondered if they would make it to October. Shortly after October there would be Christmas and, if this did not kill them, another mean year beyond. For the first time in at least twenty years he wished that God was still a problem he could believe in. He needed something solid to crash into, something beyond himself to blame. Lowering his weight to the floor he sat cross-legged amongst their wellington boots and tennis racquets. He reminded himself that it was not in his job description to fold under this or any other disappointment.

I must put my wife first, he told himself firmly. *I am here to look after her.* But his feet did not move and his shoulders showed no inclination towards leaving the cloakroom.

When he was a child, his mother had often dragged him along on her weekly shopping trips. Though money was tight and she'd rarely bought anything which could not be eaten or used in some practical manner, she'd liked to pat clothes in British Homes Stores and C&A. Occasionally she'd left him sitting beside her handbag and the carrier bags containing the evening's dinner whilst she darted into the store's dressing rooms to try on skirts and fabulous blouses she could not afford, even at Christmas. 'Don't be telling your dad,' she'd say, and Steven never had. He'd been old enough to understand that adults kept secrets from one another: his grandfather's cigarettes, his mother's lonely moments in the Marks and Spencer's changing room, the lady his father kept for typing and other important jobs. These secrets were not the same as lies.

While his mother paraded up and down in front of the dressing-room mirrors, young Steven liked to crawl between the clothes racks in the children's department and hide for as long as he could, holding his breath against discovery. He'd grown particularly fond of bathrobes, the way they furred against his face and arms like soft toys, whispering. Also, little girls' frocks, for the rustling noise they made as they settled back into position. Perched on the metal bar which held these clothes racks together, only his feet remained visible to other shoppers and Steven could pretend that he'd slipped the seams of this world, arriving some-where strange and far removed from 1970s Northern Ireland. He had not the faith necessary to believe in Narnia and could only stretch his imagination as far as Disneyland or the Butlins' holiday resort he'd once seen in a brochure at the travel agents.

As their coats and anoraks swung gently backwards and forwards, grazing his shoulders like a blessing deferred, Steven felt, for a brief moment, insulated from the previous day's events. He had not slept properly in almost three days. The desire to close his eyes and sleep for an hour or so began to blur his resolve. *Just for a second*, he told himself and, leaning against his golf bag, allowed his eyelids to droop. He was just beginning to forget his wife when the sounds of loud drums and synthesizers, came rushing through the air-conditioning vents and he was all of a sudden bolt upright, crowning his head on the coat rail.

Outside the cloakroom the music was just as persistent. Without the muffled protection of coats and winter scarves he could hear actual voices, laughter and singing, rising through the floorboards from the apartment below.

The rooms directly below their own apartment were occupied by another, much younger couple. He was English and the crass donkey bray of his laughter often rose to greet Steven and his wife first thing in the morning and late at night. She had been raised in Belfast and they'd met, quite accidentally, during her studies in Edinburgh. This couple were planning to be married in the spring, after which they would wait at least two years before getting pregnant. There were things they wished to do around the house before a baby arrived and holidays to be taken in Italy and Greece. Steven and his wife knew more about this couple than they did about their own in-laws. They were the sort of forward people who wished to know their neighbours and cornered them for fresh news in the stairwells and corridors. That which they had not been told directly they'd gleaned in snippets and loud exclamations, as the young couple's conversations rose like warm air through their own ceiling and into Steven's apartment.

They were not the sort of young couple who held house parties, and this, Steven often reminded his wife, was something to be thankful for. However, they often, even on weeknights, had eight or more friends round for dinner. The noise of this was almost as unbearable as an actual house party. Steven could feel the hammers rising inside his gut. To play music on a night like this was absolutely inexcusable and, though he acknowledged in the small part of his mind which was still working logically that these neighbours could not possibly know, he still intended to go downstairs and shout at them loudly, through the letterbox, if they would not open their door.

Steven was just striding towards his own front door, reminding himself as he approached the doormat to grab his shoes, when he heard his wife calling his name from the living room. 'Steven,' she said, 'come here a minute.' He stopped by the open door and peered into the living room. There was still no sign of his wife but he could hear her shallow breathing like tissue paper rising and falling in the breeze. He stepped into the room, shuffled across the carpet and, having arrived at the coffee table, saw her naked feet protruding from behind the sofa. Her ankles were thin and porcelain white, the blue lines of her veins glowing through the skin like the luminous workings of a just-born bird. He was seized by the inclination to wrap his hands around her ankles and hold her down, lest she suddenly float away.

He hunkered down beside her feet and peeked around the corner of the sofa to make sure the rest of her was still there. She was lying sideways on the floor, knees curled into her belly, right ear pressed into the carpet, whilst her right arm and hand hooked the dead space above her head. He wondered if this was coincidental of if she'd consciously put herself into the recovery position. He placed a single hand lightly on the spot where her pyjamas had crawled up, exposing a foot or more of milky shin. She was warm to the touch and this surprised him. He was about to open his mouth and offer toast or ask if she was OK when she raised herself up on one elbow and held a finger to her lips, shooshing him like a fussy child. Curling her finger into a clothes hook, she beckoned for Steven to come and lie down beside her.

This was the first and only thing she'd asked of him in almost three days and so without so much as a heartbeat of hesitation, he put his shoulder to the sofa, shoved it into the coffee table and dropped down beside her. They lay face to face together like forks in a cutlery drawer. He was not touching her with any part of his body or clothes. He could smell her breath, stale from yesterday's coffee and too much sleep. On the floor, with his wife's eyes heavy upon him, Steven felt a separate kind of grief settle into his bones. He belted his arms across his ribcage, drew his kneecaps up to meet his chin and tried, as best he could, to hold himself together.

'Listen,' said his wife, 'they're playing music downstairs.'

There was no joy left in her, but the ghost of something which might in a month's or several months' time become a smile went flitting across her eyes like a dark-night moth. He understood then that they should not aim for Christmas or even October; the following morning would be mountain enough for them to conquer. He allowed his ear to fall heavily upon the carpet, to find the noise of the couple in the apartment below and press into it, splitting the sound, as it bubbled up through the floorboards, into individual components: laughter, music and passionate conversation.

'Someone's still happy,' she said. They lay like this for hours, until their ears grew numb and their tea lost its heat. Around two, the couple in the apartment below fell silent, but they lay on, unwilling to sleep or to rise from the floor. It was easier this way. If they slept, they would eventually wake, and it would be morning or perhaps afternoon – a new day, moving forwards. They were not ready for tomorrow. They were not ready for any of this.

12.

Shopping

In October I began a love affair with a man named either John or Paul.

We met once a week on Tuesdays by arranged accident in Knocknagoney Tesco. (It would have been more convenient to meet in the Connswater store but they did not have a café and dinner was the only active element in our relationship.)

We were careful to arrive alone: him first and me three to five minutes later, clutching a handful of carrier bags like the ghost of a crumpled alibi. We sat at a table by the condiment station and ate our dinner off plastic trays still sweating from the dishwasher steam. I was a vegetarian by birth, yet in his company rode a rare carnivorous streak through steaks, sausage rolls and reconstituted-chicken products. At the time I enjoyed the sensation of flesh resisting teeth in that stringsome, sinewy fashion rarely found in vegetables. Afterwards, I vomited in the car park, discretely, by the trolley station. The colour of it was brown and red and burgundy-brown as it pooled on the greasy tarmac. Poking through this muck-toned mess, I discovered that evil things had grown inside me and were leaking out: doubts, lies, premeditated lust and an

almost insatiable appetite for cocktail sausages. On the drive
home I picked the last of it from between my teeth with the
corner of my Tesco loyalty card. The taste persisted, requiring
the attention of toothpaste and medicated mouthwash.

Our love affair lasted for approximately eight months, peter-
ing out and finally ending towards the middle of May, just as the
city was beginning her annual attempt at good weather. Though
I did not feel particularly guilty from one Tuesday to the next, I
found myself wondering about the contents of his fridge every
time I opened my own. Medium cheddar, I presumed, for I'd
watched him buy it every week, by the half pound, along with
tomatoes on the vine, iceberg lettuce and three litres of semi-
skimmed: a cold, wet monument to an unmentioned other, waiting
at home with a bowl of dehydrated muesli.

We did not talk about our other lives. We did not talk or even
look directly at each other. We hoped the other diners would
ignore the very many empty tables circling the walls of the café
and suppose us thrown together by chance and spatial limitations.
Traditionally, I took the north-east corner of the table and he,
the south-west. We were compass points, straining for a good-
sense separation. Even after a month, we did not talk and seldom
broke the silence which sat between us like a second cousin once
removed.

'Is this seat taken?' I asked the first time I saw him. He was
the only person eating alone in the café at the Knocknagoney
Tesco. At first I felt sorry for him and thought we might talk
about the rain or the road works on the Sydenham Bypass. Then
I became attracted to his sweater and the way he held his fork,
high and adamant, like an American film star. When he spoke,
his accent was almost entirely East Belfast. I was disappointed
and also reassured. It was a relief of sorts to find we spoke the
same dull, doughy language.

He told me his name was John or perhaps Paul. (Distracted by the ring on his last but one finger I could never remember his name, but retained a vague awareness that he was named for a Beatle, and not a minor one.)

I offered my name and asked what he did. He never replied. I presumed him a teacher or a civil servant. He had the shoes for it, also a nervous habit of running his hands through the back of his hair in erratic tugs and spurts as if being subjected to a series of small electric shocks. He was not a handsome man but he knew how to wear a sweater.

'Do you want to have a love affair with me?' he asked. In all my years of shopping at Knocknagoney Tesco, I had never once been asked this question. It felt impolite to refuse. I might never be asked again.

'I only come here on Tuesdays,' I replied. 'Wouldn't you like someone more committed?'

'Tuesdays suit me fine,' he answered, 'I can get the groceries while we're having our affair.'

It was a perfect storm. We shook on it, our hands finding each other across the table top. Though I did not realise it at the time, it was to be the longest and most intimate conversation of our relationship.

We always began with dinner in the café. Anxious not to raise suspicions, I ate before leaving home and ate again in his presence, the second dinner sitting like a beached beluga in the pit of my belly. I was almost always bloated in his company, and on Tuesdays wore loose-fitting shirts and jumpers, hoping he would not presume me pregnant. An unplanned pregnancy was the last thing our love affair needed. I bought my own dinner. He bought his. We were, in this and other matters, terribly modern. Later, when we'd grown accustomed to one another and familiarity had made us daring, we used vouchers – two for one on fish and chips or cardboard-crusted quiche – splitting the cost of a single meal concisely and alternating on the leftover penny.

We were just as frugal with our affections.

'I find you almost as attractive as my wife,' he said on our second date.

'You have slightly better legs than her,' on our third.

Words were cheap. We rarely touched.

After dinner we walked the aisles of the supermarket, colliding surreptitiously on every other corner. It was a joy and a horror of sorts to round the vegetable aisle and find him lingering by the closed-cap mushrooms, daring me to drive my trolley hard into his ankles.

'Sorry,' we said, and neither party was sorry, only thrilled and slightly frustrated by the anoraks, the cardigans and the weekday underwear which conspired against us and could not be removed in a supermarket setting. There were other ways to collide, of course. We bought the same kind of marmalade and the same kind of bread and agreed to think lustful thoughts over our individual slices of breakfast toast. (I could not bring myself to tell him that marmalade was ugly to me and the only thing I could bear on toast was margarine. I ate my toast dry for a week and felt like an unfaithful lover.) The situation escalated. Marmalade was not enough to keep us together.

'I want to do things to you,' I whispered over the magazine racks one evening.

'Me too,' he replied, 'but I've also got to get the shopping done.'

We came to a very practical compromise, an austere kind of give and take which was much better than marmalade, but far from best.

I placed individual items in his trolley. He placed different items in mine. Little bits of each other breaching the sanctity of personal space like the stray socks and hair slides which slip down the side of a lover's bed. We left it longer and longer before removing these items, often stacking them on the side of the checkout, too shit-scared to risk the questions which would come from carrying home an uncharacteristic pineapple or hair-care product.

'It seems odd that we never touch,' I finally admitted, and he pointed out that this was my first supermarket love affair and perhaps I was confusing it with a more pedestrian kind of arrangement. I had to agree that he was right, though my fingers and my knees and the small of my back throbbed in protest.

'It's not that we can't touch,' he explained, 'it's just that there are different rules in supermarkets.'

And so we allowed our hands to brush and linger in the dairy aisle. It was easiest in the dairy aisle, for everyone buys milk and butter and at least one kind of cheese. Reaching through the early evening crush for a strawberry yogurt or half pint of cream, even the most intimate gesture could pass as accidental. We fell into each other when the aisles were quiet and, on all other occasions, feigned clumsiness. He could hesitate between one brand of butter and another for almost a minute, fingers darting backwards and forwards across the shelf so that our elbows clashed and separated and met again like the fickle undulations of an evening tide. I rolled my sleeves to the elbow and always went for the milk at the back of the shelf. And, if my reward was a two-second rush of forearm freckling against chilled forearm, I paid for it in next-day use-bys and wasted milk.

We never forgot, even for one heady second, that the shopping came first. It would have been ludicrous to return home without the hand soap or the mandarin oranges we'd set out for. Questions would have been asked. We brought shopping lists to guard against distraction; his was slightly longer than mine, so I suspected children, at least two, possibly three. On the best Tuesdays

– when he wore the red pullover and I chanced heels – the lists were the only things which kept us anchored to the supermarket floor.

Towards the end of May, when our love affair was approaching its seventh shy month, he said, 'Let's go crazy tonight. It's too hot for good sense.'

I thought he might kiss me. I had yet to see the inside of his mouth.

Instead, he ordered salad in the café and soft drinks in lieu of our usual coffees. After dinner, he tidied our trays away, careful to recycle the recyclable elements. He reminded me of my father, or perhaps my father's father, and this was a nervous shrug of a feeling, not so far removed from a common cold. He wasn't even wearing the red sweater. In light of this and other dull decisions, I felt inclined to draw a line under the whole love affair.

'Things need to change,' I said, as we collected our trolleys, 'this isn't working for me.'

'Things can change,' he said. When we arrived in the frozen-desserts aisle he took leave of himself and grabbed me by the wrists, forcefully. He left marks: four red lines and a dot, circling each arm like a bracelet. I studied my wrists for a week, watching as the red bruised into blue and finally brown. It was the only thing he'd ever given me and, for days after, I prodded the marks with a blunt pencil, hoping to get another week out of the bruises. It was a giddy thing to be grabbed by him in full view of the Arctic rolls. I forgot that we were a modern couple and that my arms were my own to fold and withdraw. I forgot about the groceries and the shopping list and the carefully clipped vouchers tucked inside my purse. My wrists said, 'Boy, oh boy it's really happening now,' for he'd never grabbed at any part of me before. My ankles were keen to get in on the action. I leant backwards and forwards, anticipating any amount of craziness.

'Watch this,' he said, and opening the freezer door, selected a box of milk chocolate Magnum ice creams. 'Let's be spontaneous. We'll eat them right here in the aisle.'

'But they're not even on the shopping list,' I gasped, thrilled by the way he was ripping the cardboard wrapper off.

'I know,' he said, 'and we haven't paid for them yet.'

'But we will, won't we?'

'Of course we will. We may be crazy, but we're not degenerates. I'll keep the box.'

He turned the box upside down and emptied the contents into his hands. There were three ice creams in total. It was like first communion. He passed one to me, took one for himself and seemed unsure what to do with the third.

'I didn't think there would be three,' he said.

'There's always three Magnums in a pack,' I replied. 'We usually have one each and put one in the icebox for later.'

It was entirely the wrong thing to say. 'We' was not the once-a-week-on-Tuesdays exception but rather the rule, my pronoun of habit and ten years next spring. He looked at the extra Magnum, still white with freezer fur, and he thought about his own icebox and his wife, and his two or possibly three children. I could see these thoughts as they folded into his forehead, forming train tracks and telephone wires from one sad conclusion to the next. All the craziness drained out of him. Under the strip lights, with a handful of thawing ice creams, he was no longer dangerous or remarkable. He was a civil servant in a BHS pullover, getting the groceries in. He was somebody's husband, much like my own, but thinner.

'I need to pick up some washing powder,' he said, and we both knew that the washing-powder aisle was on the other side of the building, as far removed as the supermarket would allow. It was the last thing he ever said to me. The following Tuesday I made my excuses and began buying our groceries at Asda. (Things were cheaper in Asda, and there was little chance of seeing him, but the vegetables never lasted as long.)

After he'd left, I lingered in the frozen-desserts aisle. It seemed appropriate. I ate my Magnum slowly, peeling the chocolate off with the edge of a fingernail. I took small pleasure in the fact that the box was in his trolley. As he approached the checkout and paid for his washing powder and medium cheddar, he'd find himself – for the first and last time – buying me dinner: the only concrete sin in an otherwise sinless love affair.

13.

Alternative Units

'Hey Liz,' you say, 'did you see the house is up for sale again?'

You have purposefully waited till my mouth is full of sandwich to say this.

'Hrmmm,' I say through bacon, lettuce, tomato and artisan rye. Bread is not a quick chew, like rice or pasta. You have at least ninety seconds of my silence in which to present your argument. It is an argument I have heard many times before. In the past I've always said, 'No,' and, 'Definitely not,' and other stronger sentiments, usually with swearing.

I will not be swearing today. Freddy is with us. He is here beneath the tablecloth, twisting himself round the legs of the restaurant chairs. I can feel the heat of his small body sweating against my shins as he winds his way from one end of the table to the other. The brush of him, barely there and then gone, makes me think of little fish flitting beneath boats and ocean swimmers. On the other side of the table, an untouched toastie marks the place where he should be sitting. Melted cheese drips from the bread like tears turning solid as they cool. You say I need to stop ordering food for Freddy in restaurants. It is a waste of money. We do not have money to waste. I can see the waitresses thinking this with their eyes when they come to lift the plates and Freddy's is untouched.

'Finished with this?' they'll ask. I'll say, 'Uh huh, he's not that hungry today,' and you'll catch the waitress knowingly by the eye, and maybe, if you think I'm not looking, chance a shoulder shrug.

I find this very offensive, John. It is like you are making a team with the waitress and I am not on this team even though I should be. We are still married. Despite everything, we are still Freddy's parents. I have told you more times than I can remember that we need to operate as a unit. You cannot be making other, alternative units with waitresses or sisters or, for that matter, therapists. I have used various metaphors to explain this to you: for example, singing from the same hymn sheet, presenting a united front and being in it together for the long run (which is actually two separate sayings pressed together for effect).

You always tell me that this is different. That this is not about working together or not working together. This is just about being sensible.

'Sensible!' I fire back at you, my voice coming dangerously close to shattering. 'You want to talk about sensible? Tell me, John, is it sensible to make your family move out of the house they love, all the way across town, to a rickety old house you haven't lived in since you were ten?'

'I was happy in that house,' you say. 'I think we could be happy in that house again.'

I ignore you every time you talk about happiness. Your idea of happiness is like the outline of a circle. My idea of happiness is all the parts huddled together in the middle. We used to complement each other perfectly. Since Freddy, we don't.

'It's only you that wants to move,' I say. 'I'm quite happy where I am and I'm certain Freddy doesn't want to move either.

He might not even come with us if we left our house. It's not sensible, John. It's just plain selfish.' This will be the final word in the argument about houses, until the next time you bring it up.

Last Friday the house went up for sale again.

Straightaway I knew this had happened. It was all in with the way you walked into the kitchen after work. Your voice was going, 'Things are looking up,' and, 'It's getting better all the time,' but your mouth wasn't buying any of its bullshit.

You are not subtle when you want something, John. If you don't ask outright you make it clear with your feet. Once, you stumped round the house so loudly I phoned the Internet company and paid for superfast broadband before you even had the chance to ask for it. Another time I let you get me pregnant though I did not want another baby in the house. Freddy is enough for me. But your hands, and the way they touched me – like tiny cattle prods, pushing, pushing, pushing – made it quite clear he was not enough for you.

Oh, you are definitely not subtle when you want something.

When we first met I could not get enough of this. The way you looked at me as if I was something to be eaten or unpeeled. Now I am tired and wish to be held like a hardboiled egg still in its shell. You do not want me like this. You do not even want to eat me or unpeel me any more. You only want me to be sensible like the wives of your colleagues and brothers.

'Why can't you be sensible about this, Liz?' you ask. 'It's been four years now.' You are meaning everything from the house to the way I wear my hair and all my grandmother's jewellery at once. You are mostly meaning how I am with Freddy.

You think the house will help with Freddy. You think it will be a new start for the two of us and the baby which you put inside me. These are the out-loud reasons you give me for moving. Inside, I know you are hoping we can leave Freddy behind.

You are hoping that the new baby will be Freddy without any of the unfortunate parts. You are not a bad man. You may not even realise that you are thinking these terrible thoughts. But I know you are.

I have seen the *Property News* circled on your desk and the brochure from the estate agent that you have left by the downstairs toilet, waiting for me to find it there, smirking. Now, we are in a lunch place about to have the house argument again, and I am using my ninety seconds of chewing to remind myself not to cause a scene, or swear in front of Freddy. It is important not to upset him. He is always with me but even now, after four years, I still worry that he will tire of me and leave. I am his mother. We should be like magnets, joined at the hip, peas in a pod, Tweedle-dum and Tweedledee. When he was very little we were inseparable. I wore him bandaged against my chest and when he cried, felt the sob of it in my lungs, like a kind of premonition. I cannot be sure how close we are now. Do magnets lose their pull with time? This is a serious question I am asking you, John. You have always been more scientific than me.

Freddy is not listening to us this afternoon. He is under the table making small mountains of other people's crumbs. He likes to do this in restaurants. I should stop him. It's unhygienic. But he tells me it is just like building sandcastles and, as we do not have a beach in this town, or even a sandpit at the park, I say, 'what the hell, let the child play with other people's crumbs. There are worse things he could be doing.'

While I am chewing, I peek under the table and smile at him. He is using the corner of his hand as a shovel, scraping pizza crusts, breadcrumbs and tiny slivers of grated cheese into a pile. He smiles back at me and gives me a thumbs up. Freddy no longer speaks but I understand what he means. I do telepathy on him with my mind. *Do you want to go and live in Gran Gran's old house?*

I ask him and he replies, *No way, Jose. I like our house just fine.* I am glad that we can talk to each other without words. It is perfect for situations like this, when my mouth is full.

You do not talk to Freddy any more. At first you did. You were better at the talking than I was. You called him, 'Wee mate,' and 'Bud.' You told him he was breaking your heart and also breaking my heart – both our hearts really, because back then our hearts could not be separated out. You were usually crying when you talked to Freddy. The therapist said crying was good and extremely healthy. She also said writing things down was good. Then, after a year, she said that it would be good to start thinking about the future. 'No thank you,' I said, but you stopped crying and you stopped writing things down. Then you stopped talking to Freddy altogether. You asked the hairdresser to cut your hair differently. This was how normal people showed the world they were making a new start. I had not seen any of this coming. It was like a car accident.

'What's the point in talking to him?' you asked. 'It's not like he hears me. It's not like he ever replies.'

You wouldn't even say his name out loud.

It wasn't just Freddy you stopped speaking to. You barely had anything to say to me: only bills and if we were running low on milk or bread. We kept acting the part of two people who were leaning against each other. This was easier than telling our friends we were over. We fell asleep side by side in the same bed. When I woke up you were always on the sofa and I'd wonder how long you'd waited before leaving me. You went back to work and I didn't. You started jogging, stopped drinking, looked up package holidays on the Internet. I didn't. I hated you for thinking about the future. I couldn't say this without leaving you. Leaving you was not an option. There was Freddy to consider and I had no money of my own. You were the one with the proper job.

I swallow the chewed-up sandwich. It sticks in my throat and I take a mouthful of water to shift it.

'Freddy's under the table building crummy castles,' I say.

'Crummy castles' is a phrase we came up with years ago, when Freddy was just a toddler and already making piles out of other people's food. It used to make you smile. Sometimes you even laughed. You are not laughing now.

'Don't be cross,' I say. 'I know it's unhygienic. I'll make him wash his hands before we leave.'

'Freddy doesn't want to move house,' I say.

It's as if you have been waiting for me to say the third of these sentences. It is like we are reading from a kind of script. Now it is your turn to respond.

'Freddy's not under the table,' you say.

'He is. I can feel him leaning against my ankles.'

'Freddy's dead, Liz,' you say. You used to say this kindly. Now you say it like a hammer. You are loud. You are very, very loud and people at other tables are turning to look at us.

'Shhh,' I whisper, 'I know that Freddy's dead. We've been over this a hundred times. He's still here though. Look under the table, John. See for yourself.'

You refuse to look. You refuse to admit that our son is still here, building sandcastles and running through the sprinkler in the backyard, watching cartoons on the living-room sofa and crawling into bed between us when he cannot sleep. It is easier for you to say he is dead than lift the tablecloth and look at him down there, grinning.

'Jesus, Liz, you have to give this up. '

'Don't swear,' I say, 'not in front of Freddy.'

We have made a pact not to swear or shout at one another in his presence. It is a pact from the time before, but I insist that it still holds. Mostly we manage to keep to the no-shouting rule or, if we can't keep our mouths kind, I put him to bed early and we go at each other as quietly as possible in the kitchen, with the door pulled shut. When we are having our Freddy-might-hear arguments, our voices are like water forced down a tube, which is to say, they are strong and insistent, capable of lifting skin.

You are holding your head in your hands now, leaning your elbows on the tablecloth. A smudge of relish has attached itself to the cuff of your shirt. It is brown and a little lumpy. I should reach over and wipe it off with a napkin or at very least tell you it is there. I don't. It makes me feel superior to look at the stain and know you have not yet noticed it. I'm not sure why I feel like this. It will be me who washes your shirt later and that stain will need bleaching.

'Listen,' I say, 'I didn't ask for a ghost child. It's not an ideal situation. But you're still his father. I'm still his mother, and I don't think I have it in me to turn my back on him.'

You don't reply. Your face is moving up and down slowly inside your hands. At first I think you are chewing a bite of hamburger, but you have no hamburger left to eat. Then, I notice that there is water on your plate, puddling through the crumbs and the greased streaks of burger relish. You are crying. This is a new thing. You don't allow yourself to cry any more.

I reach across the table, past the menu holder and the condiment bottles. I put my hand on your hand. It is colder than I'd expected. Our hands lying on the table look like the hands of dead people, folded across dead peoples' chests. You do not move your hand. In the past you pulled away when I tried to touch you. Today you don't.

'Look John, I'll move,' I say. 'If it's this important to you then sell the house and buy your old house. I'll go with you, under one condition.'

You raise your head and look straight at me. I can see where the tears have left lines on your cheeks. Your skin is dry these days and there are tiny circles of eczema in the hinged part of your elbows. This is from the stress. (I have stomach cramps and the hair is thin enough on my crown to see scalp pinking below.) You are still handsome even when you are crying, even when you have eczema. You are handsome and sad like Eastern European men in movies. You look at me hard. Your eyebrows are all up at the edges as if you are asking me a question.

'What's the condition?' you ask.

'You need to get Freddy to move with us.'

'Liz, please.'

'That's my only condition.'

'Freddy's dead.'

'That may be, John but he's still with us, and I'm not moving anywhere without him.'

You take your hand back. You look at the palm of it, then the fingers and the fingernails. Eventually you shrug and say, 'OK, if that's what it takes, I'll ask Freddy if he wants to move with us.'

You look like a man who has been driving a truck all night by himself. You go to stand up, unhooking your jacket from the back of the chair.

'Do it now,' I say.

'Here, in the restaurant?'

'No time like the present.'

'People might hear.'

'People be damned. People don't have to deal with the kind of shit we have to deal with every day. Ask him right now.'

'Freddy do you want to move house with us?' you mumble into the napkin dispenser.

'He's not at the table, John. He's under the table,' I say. I make a pointing finger and use it to point towards the place where

Freddy is making his crummy castle beneath the tablecloth. I am kind of enjoying this. I am hating every minute of it.

You swear under your breath, something vaguely Catholic. Then, you lift the edge of the tablecloth and duck your head under the table as if you are looking for a dropped phone.

'Freddy,' you say, 'do you want to move to a new house with us?' I can hear you through the table and the tablecloth. I can hear your disbelief louder than your words. You are not even using the right voice for children. You are using a voice for people with learning difficulties or grandparents, just before they die.

You lift your head. The tablecloth is caught on the back of your neck so you are wearing it like a shroud, like the Virgin Mary. I reach across the table and gently detach it. You are crying again.

'Well?' I ask.

'He says yes,' you reply. 'He says he'll move house with us.'

I know this is a lie because Freddy does not say anything any more, but I haven't the stomach for another argument.

Then, the waitress is here beside us. She asks, 'Is everything all right?' and you say, 'Yes, I just dropped my mobile.' When she lifts Freddy's untouched toastie, you say, 'Sorry, he's not that hungry today,' and I feel like something has come between us again and it is a kind of glue. I do not want to move into the house where you grew up, but I will if it means we can be a team again and Freddy can be part of this team too.

'I think the new house will be good for us,' I say. This is what you really want to hear. I offer you my hand and you take it. Under the table I am reaching for Freddy's hand. We are all three joined together in a chain but you cannot see Freddy and Freddy cannot see you.

By the time you get round to bidding on the house it has already gone out of our price range.

You call the estate agent yourself and make a point of saying,

'I grew up in that house. It's special to me.' Special means nothing to the estate agent. He only speaks money and we do not have the extra ten thousand required to outbid our rivals. When you start talking about how important the house is and how it will be a new start for us after a very hard time, it is like you are speaking French and the estate agent cannot understand a word of French. I can hear his silence from the other side of the kitchen. He is trying to make you hang up with his mind.

After you hang up the telephone you go sit in the corner of the kitchen, hunkered down between the fridge and the back door. You hold your head in both your hands as if it is too heavy for your shoulders. I am afraid to touch you. This is not the fear of being hit. It is more like the fear of being stung.

'Oh well,' I say, 'it wasn't meant to be.'

I make you magic pie for dinner. This has been your favourite dinner since you were around eight years old and your mother invented it from leftover sausages and mashed potato. The magic pie is a bad idea. It reminds you of the house you grew up in and the way you used to sit at the kitchen table, picking the beans out with a teaspoon so they lasted longer.

You are very angry in a quiet way. Your anger is like clean drinking glasses stacked top to bottom in a tower. It is shrill. I am afraid to brush against your anger. I am afraid to make even the smallest noise in its presence.

Freddy is in the utility room going through the laundry basket for odd socks. He likes to stuff eggs into the toes of socks. He has been doing this for years now, hoping the heat will hatch a chicken. He knows there is a link between chickens and keeping an egg warm. This is your fault for borrowing that book about farm animals from the library, the one which was intended for adults, not small children. For a city kid, Freddy has always known far too much about livestock. I was afraid he'd turn out to be a vegetarian. This is not the worst thing a person can become but it is sometimes awkward at dinner parties. Now he is dead I do not have to worry about this or about keeping him clean or well-slept. Having a ghost child is about fifty percent less work than having a real child. No one told me this at the funeral. It wouldn't have been appropriate.

I go into the utility room and close the door gently behind me.

'Daddy's having a bad day,' I say, 'we should probably just stay in here and keep quiet till he feels better.'

Freddy smiles at me. He is no different than he was before. I'd always imagined ghosts as pale creatures, but he is, if anything, the brightest he's ever been. He still has the tan lines and freckles from our holiday in France, and his hair is almost white-blond with the sun. He is always wearing the same outfit: red shorts and a blue shirt with thin black lines hooping around his belly. He does not wear shoes and his feet are without lines or flaws of any kind. He is like a postcard from our last good holiday. We have not taken any holidays since; we have not even been to the beach. You find the ocean too much water to manage in one place.

Freddy shuffles over to make room for me on the floor. He hands me a sports sock, greying at the toe and heel. I hunker down beside him on the cold lino. It smells of laundry in this room. It always does. I reach for an egg from the carton and care-fully palm it into my sock, doubling the cuff over so it cannot slip out. Freddy is doing the same with a black dress sock. We line our socks up next to each other on a folded-over towel. Gently, gently so the shells do not crack. It is a kind of surgery. We are happy to do this without talking. Sometimes my hand catches against Freddy's hand and it is not cold like the hand of a corpse. It is lukewarm, like water coming out of a tap last thing at night.

While we are wrapping our eggs and I am humming a kind of work song (possibly Elton John, possibly Radiohead), you are in the kitchen ruining everything. You are phoning up the estate agent and saying, 'Look here, if we can't buy the special house, the one I grew up in, then what's the closest house to it that we can buy?'

The estate agent is speaking the same language as you now. He says, 'I understand, sir. It's a great neighbourhood isn't it? There are good schools in the area too. For your ten thousand less than the original house I could easily sell you the house next door.'

'Done,' you say. You are so desperate to be close to the place you want to live that you do not even ask what sort of a house you are buying.

It will turn out to be a small white house with a swing in the back garden and three bedrooms: one for us, one for the new baby and one which I will call Freddy's room and you will call the guest room, as if our son is an old college friend you have invited to stay for the weekend. You will pace the fence of this house nightly, watching the lights blond off and on in the house where you grew up. You will imagine they are laughing at you.

'We could have been happy again in that house,' you will say. The near miss of this will be your excuse for ignoring the young couple who live in the house now. You will also ignore their dogs and their cats and their happy future children. You will pretend not to see them in the drive when you are backing the car out. You will throw their undelivered Amazon parcels in the bin, despite what you promised the postman. You will not blow their leaves. You will not lend them milk. You will not trim their side of the hedge, though it is an effort on your part to leave their bit untidy.

You will go through their rubbish at night with a torch, separating scraps of wallpaper, taps, bathroom tiles, lampshades and door handles from the everyday detritus of their life. You will keep these items, carefully labelled in plastic tubs which you will buy from Ikea particularly for this purpose.

'Someday,' you will say, 'those dreadful people will move out. Then we can buy the house I grew up in. Then we can be happy again.'

I will nod towards the Ikea tubs stacked in the corner of the utility room. 'Are you planning on putting all those handles and windows and rusty kitchen taps back into the house?' I'll ask.

You will look at me like we are on the same team again and say, 'It's got to be exactly the same as it used to be, Liz.' You might even rest your hand on the round of my belly where the next baby is starting to swell. This will feel like the kind of bandage which has been put on too tight.

I will stand in the kitchen of our new white house, beside the sink, where I can clearly see the house you grew up in. Freddy might be there with us, beneath the table or under one of the chairs, because being under things will make him feel safer in the new house.

'This is not the place I want to be,' I will say, and you will reply, 'This is not the place I want to be, either.' If Freddy is still with us, he will be saying exactly the same thing from his spot, beneath the table. He won't be using out-loud words, but I will still be able to hear him with my mind.

I will wonder how we got here and how long we'll have to stay in this place, which is like a motorway service station, which is like a not-very-good compromise, which is like a thing you say at the end of an argument when you are too tired and should not be saying anything at all.

But, all of this is many, many months away. Right now, you are still on the phone with the estate agent, ruining everything.

With one hand, I am holding the door closed between us. I

do not want you in here with Freddy and me – you and your stupid trying to move on. I am quite content to stay here. On our side of the door everything is not ruined yet. On our side of the door we are putting eggs inside socks, as we often do at the week-end.

We are concentrating. We are quiet in each other's company. We are brave and happy. Then, you shout through from the kitchen, 'Liz, come out here. We've bought a house.' Freddy drops the sock he is holding and the egg cracks as it hits the floor. He makes a little noise like air settling in a radiator and a thing comes between us like magnets turning against each other.

Tomorrow morning there will be a shiny mark on the lino where the egg white has crusted over. I will peel it off with the edge of my fingernails. It will come away in flakes. As I am scraping at the egg white I will think, *Here is a mark which my son has left on this house. It is not a permanent mark. There is nothing to tell his presence after we leave.* Then, I will take the edge of a cheese knife and carve the height of him into the doorframe. I will rest the knife's handle against the bone of his head and wonder if this will be the last time I feel Freddy solid beneath my hand, like a thing I cannot pass through.

14.

Dinosaur Act

For Damian Smyth

Jim died on the day before Pancake Tuesday. Sandra didn't bother with pancakes, nor did she give up anything for Lent. The loss of a husband seemed sacrifice enough. Besides, the house was full of pies and sponge cake left over from the wake.

Their friends sent sympathy cards, more than she'd expected. Sandra lined them up along the mantelpiece, moving her ornaments to make space. When the room ran out she asked their son to string a wire, and hung the cards across the wall. They'd only ever done this with cards at Christmas. The effect was too jolly for a death. Her daughters told her so, suggesting that the sympathy cards be moved to the dining room, where they wouldn't be so demanding. Sandra didn't listen to them. She liked the way the strung cards lifted in the breeze each time the door opened. Something is settling, she thought, and folded her arms accordingly.

After Jim died, people came to sit quietly on Sandra's sofa. They balanced her good cups and saucers on their thighs. Some of the women cried. They expected nothing of her. This was not true. They expected sandwiches, strong tea and a measured grief, neither too hot nor too cold to credit the loss of a just-retired husband. Sandra delivered all this and sausage rolls on an Evesham platter. She was good with death. All four of their parents had passed away in the last few years. The language of wake and burial still lingered at the back of her tongue, loose as holiday Spanish.

For three days, Sandra opened her door to neighbours, family friends and relatives who'd driven from Ballymena and Tandragee just to say they were sorry and drive straight home again. 'I'm sorry for your loss,' they said, and Sandra replied, 'Thank you.' She wished there was a script for such conversations and, at the same time, understood that liturgy made her feel awkward, as if her teeth were too large for her own mouth. On Easter Sundays, when the minister announced, 'He is risen,' she could never bring herself to reply, 'He is risen, indeed.' Instead, she smiled and stared into the gallery, fixating on the spot where the paint was peeling off in the shape of a bird. She hoped no one would mistake her silence for apostasy. For this, and other reasons, Sandra could never have been a Catholic.

She wasn't cut out for duty either. If Jim had not anchored her into it, she'd never have visited the dead or dying, never have gone round to commiserate with any of their more unfortunate friends. Jim had always known exactly how to approach a sadness. Sandra sat quietly by his side, nodding. 'We're praying for you, especially at the minute,' she'd say, if a statement was required of her. She meant every word, but could not have elaborated on the theme. She hugged the women like they were once again children, and shook the hands of the men lightly as if holding a particularly fragile plate. She brought chicken-and-ham pie in a tinfoil dish; home-made, not shop-bought. Afterwards, they could bin the dish. This seemed to be what people required of her. She was known to be good in a crisis. This was not true. Jim was good in a crisis, and Sandra was extremely good at standing next to him.

In the days following Jim's death, Sandra could see that other people were equally shy of loss. She watched them filing in and out of her front room. She recognised herself in the way they held their mouths oddly, as if unsure whether to laugh or spit. People who could not fully speak their sympathy baked it into fruit loaves and flakemeal biscuits. They left their cake tins, without saying, in towering stacks on her kitchen counter. Some of them were labelled with handwritten names: Mrs Adger, Mrs McKeown, June McNeilly. Sandra wasn't sure if this meant they wanted their tins back, and, if so, how long she should wait after the funeral to return them. There was too much cake for one person, and the freezer was still full from Christmas.

Several of Jim's old mates from the shipyards appeared at the wake. Sandra didn't recognise any of them, but every so often recalled a name in passing, the memory of it hooking at her grief as she remembered an anecdote Jim had once passed across their dinner table, easy as a dish of boiled potatoes. They were big men with damp skin and proper suits, kept good for funerals and marching. A fair percentage of them were also called Jim or some clipped version of James. They announced themselves from the hall gruffly, as if they'd not yet grown into their names. They refused to sit, even when seats were available. 'I'm not stopping, love.' 'No tea for myself, I've just risen from a cup.' When leaving, they lingered too long in the doorway, holding one of Sandra's hands in two of theirs like they were trying to pray and forgetting the words. When they drew back to leave, as often as not, she'd find a clammy fiver or twenty-pound note marking the place where the two of them had met and parted and, in doing so, remained just as strange as ever.

Sandra would have liked for these men to cry. Every one of them was thick with the need to cry, and not just about Jim. She could see the yearning just beneath their skin. It was tight and straining like the stretched surface of a blistered heel. There was nothing she could say to provoke it. They were not the kind of men who cried, even over a dead wife – though a child might have been the exception.

The minister was equally faithful during Jim's wake. He came every day around teatime. He was a young fella, just ordained and not married. Sometimes he wore a V-neck pullover over his collar, grey or burgundy, but never patterned, even with a stripe.

'Yon fella can smell the stew from the other side of the East,' her sister said. And, sure enough, the young minister seemed to time his visits around meals. At first resisting any food the family offered and, when pressed, accepting under polite duress, a plate of something substantial.

The minister took his suit jacket off to eat, hooking it over the back of a dining-room chair. He ate like a man who lived on sandwiches, and Sandra was glad to see him fed. They'd often had this minister or one of his predecessors for Sunday lunch, and the presence of a dog collar leant an air of normalcy to their meals. Where possible, she tried to force a hot pudding on him.

'Sure, there's no harm in feeding him while he's here,' she said. 'There's more than enough to go round and he's no wife to cook for him.'

Before leaving, the young minister always read the scriptures aloud. Pushing his chair back to stand, he'd remove a black leather Bible from his breast pocket and hold it open in his right hand. He had the look of an actor when he read. The familiar funeral verses, the yea-though-I-walks, and the neither-shall-there-be-any-mournings slipped from his tongue like honeyed milk. The open Bible was only there to keep his hands occupied. This in no way diminished his appeal. This was East Belfast. People expected a minister to know the Word by heart and deliver it like a politician. After the scriptures, the minister sucked a long breath into himself so that it caught like wind at the back of his teeth. Then he raised his hands in a manner suited to a much older man. If he'd not been holding the Bible, she'd have suspected he was about to launch into some kind of dance routine.

'Folks,' he said, 'will we have a wee prayer?'

No one ever said no, though there was a different room of people every time he posed the question. No one ever said no, though half the people there hadn't darkened the door of a church in years. On the third day of the wake, Sandra felt as if she could not bear another of the minister's wet prayers, and almost spoke out in defiance.

'No thank you, Mr Cunningham. We'll not have a wee prayer after all,' she wanted to say. 'We'll have another cup of tea instead, and talk about who I'm going to go on holidays with now I've not got Jim.'

Sandra didn't say any of this. She could not even explain where this loud thought had come from. Instead, she bowed her head and closed her eyes and, on the final hallowed beat, added her own dull 'Amen' to the chorus. Afterwards, upon opening her eyes, she was shocked to find that her hands had curled into themselves, four red lines like More code running across each palm where her fingernails had dug in.

There was a lack in the house without Jim. There was an echo after the children and the children's children went home. Yet, at this, the most empty moment of her life, Sandra understood that there was no room in her for God or any of his comfort. A lone-liness slid between her and the rest of the family. It had a stiff back to it and would not bend. They were church people, and, in moments of death and serious sickness, held to their faith like drowning fish. Sandra still said all the same things the children were saying and agreed with them on everything, even the funeral hymns, yet felt herself a spectre, haunting the edges of her own living room. She tried to explain this to her son on the morning of the funeral.

'I'm finding it hard to pray,' she admitted. 'It's like there's nothing there.'

'Of course you are, Mum,' her son replied. 'You're in shock. God understands. It'll all come back to you in time.'

She was proud of their son in his funeral suit. He was the cut of his father and, under pressure, just as wise and serious. They'd brought him up for such a time as this, and here he was, more than capable: carrying the coffin, delivering the eulogy, explaining gently to her grandchildren that Grandpa was in Heaven now, with Jesus. Sandra looked at her son's big, shovelling hands as they cupped his coffee mug, and he looked older than she felt. She wished, just for this morning, that she was not his mother, but rather one of his two wee girls, still cute enough to believe everything the adults said.

He offered to pray for her right there at the kitchen table. Sandra hadn't the cruelty in her to refuse him, but his hand on her shoulder was another thing she had to carry. She barely heard him speak for wrestling with the fear that she might, at any moment, get up and leave. When her grandson came bursting through the kitchen door with a picture book and shoes to be laced, she was glad of the interruption. She scooped him up into her lap. He was four now, almost five, and really too big for lifting, but the weight of him and the angles of his wee bony backside digging into her thighs, was exactly the kind of heaviness Sandra could manage.

'I can't do my laces, Gran,' he said, and she bent in two to tie the child's feet into his new black shoes. The smell of his hair caught in her nose: chamomile and milk. He'd been bathed in preparation for the funeral.

'There you go, Sam,' she said. 'All laced up.' The unfinished prayer hung over the kitchen table like one side of an argument, never resolved.

'Grandpa's with Jesus,' the child announced. 'You shouldn't be sad, Gran.'

'Right you are, Sammy,' she said, and ruffled the child's hair so it rose, like a duck's tail, at the nape of his neck. 'Your Grandpa's happier than he's ever been right now.'

Across the table, her son smiled and nodded his assent. The child, satisfied that there was nothing here to concern himself with, returned to his picture book.

It was impossible to explain to this small, simple person all the things Sandra was currently feeling: dumb and thundering, tired as death itself. So she made her grandson hot Ribena in a mug and warned him not to spill any of it on his good white shirt. Then she opened the fridge and cried quietly into its stacked shelves, her face glowing cheerfully in the door light.

Sandra barely noticed the funeral. It happened and she watched it as if watching herself on a television programme. Everything was familiar and at the same time removed from itself. Twice she could not recall her own daughter's name in conversation. She did not cry in the church or at the graveside. She understood that this had been expected of her. Afterwards, there was no way to right it. At the grave, she stared at the coffin containing Jim and could not picture him inside. It was easier to imagine the coffin full of flat-pack furniture or electronic goods waiting to be shipped abroad. It seemed ludicrous to cover her husband in muck and walk away, as if the act of hiding him underground might somehow make the last forty years easier to forget.

For the first time, she understood why the Catholics favoured cremation. She knew a lady who'd stored her husband's remains in the pocket of her everyday handbag, tucking the old man tightly under her arm each time she left the house. This made more sense to Sandra than coffins and headstones or the polished white pebbles they'd ordered to cover Bill's plot. She knew not to mention this to any of the children. They'd inherited their grandmother's holy Protestant horror of the crematorium and would sooner have seen their father's body tipped feet first into the Lagan than burnt.

After the funeral, the young minister gave Sandra a paper booklet about bereavement. It had flowers on the front and a Bible. She recognised white lilies and gypsophila gathered in a tight, old-fashioned bunch. There was also a cross: a Protestant one, without Jesus.

'You may find that a comfort to you in the coming weeks,' the minister explained.

There were Bible verses inside and suggestions for things she could pray if she wasn't up to inventing her own prayers. Sandra slipped the booklet into the back page of her Bible and tried to forget it.

'I'm having doubts,' she said to her daughter, just one week after the funeral. 'I can't pray.'

The daughter placed a hand on Sandra's hand. Their hands were dead fish, piled up in a fishmonger's window.

'Uch, Mum, give yourself time,' she said. 'Even when you can't pray yourself, we're praying for you. God knows what you'd want to say if you could. You're just tired.'

The doctor came, on her daughter's insistence, and left tiny blue pills for the tiredness. They were diamond-shaped like the extra-strong breath mints Jim used to suck when he couldn't be bothered to brush his teeth. Sandra took them with hot milk at night and felt the blood drift heavier in her veins. She slept like a woman who had not slept in years. She dreamt of herself as a girl, left behind in an empty room, though the room changed from one night to the next and was often lifted from a television programme.

During the second week, the sleep sunk its teeth into Sandra and held on. She slept ten hours each night and still went back for a nap before dinner. She felt guilty about this and told no one. The sofa was uncomfortable for lying on, and she could not bring herself to sleep in their bed. The absence of Jim was one thing, the untouched Bible on his bedside cabinet, a beast she was not yet brave enough to confront. Sandra slept in the spare room, shoving the grandchildren's soft toys aside to make space for herself in the single bed. The bed smelt of Sam, and then her own powdery, paper smell, and, after a few weeks, stale like damp flannels dried too often. Sometimes she woke with Winnie the Pooh or Mickey cradled against her chest and cried. It was almost impossible then to get out of bed and wear slippers, to microwave something from the freezer for dinner.

'You're doing so well, Mum,' said her daughters. She looked in the mirror and knew they were only humouring her.

'Mum's not making anything of it,' they said, on their mobile phones in the hall, with the door not quite to. It was, in some frail way, comforting to have her suspicions confirmed.

Then it was almost spring. She had not noticed. Devoid of the margins created by routine, time meant very little to Sandra. The responsibility for laundry and cleaning and meals had been taken from her as if she was a child incapable of looking after herself. She rarely left the house, and never went further than Connswater Tesco, where she purchased things she did not particularly like, and let them go bad in the larder waiting for Jim's appetite to return. One of the girls always went with her. They were too polite to question any of the items Sandra placed in her trolley. She wanted them to say something. She purchased dog biscuits, tampons, vanilla essence and Radox shower gel for men, hoping to provoke a reaction. An argument would have cleaned her out in a good way, like the dull satisfaction which settles once the vomit's finally up.

Towards the end of March, Sandra noticed the nights getting a little longer. She kept the curtains open. She wondered if the lawn would soon need mowing, and who would do it now that Jim was dead? There were people you could pay to do things around the house: young, unemployed fellas, retired men looking for cash in hand and also Romanians. They could clean the windows when they were here and have a look at the guttering. There was money enough for this, and also for Christmas and holidays, if the inclination ever returned. She would ask around for recommendations and get a man in to do the garden. The decision cheered Sandra. It was the first time she hadn't consulted the children since the day of Jim's death. She'd done him a fry instead of toast that morning, and he'd grabbed her round the waist like a two-armed belt, whispering in her ear, 'What did I ever do to deserve the likes of you?'

The children would be pleased to see her making progress. Or, perhaps the children would wonder why she had not asked for their help. Her son would say, 'Uch, Mum, there was no need to pay a stranger. Sure, I can run the lawnmower over the garden any time you want.' Then Sandra would have to let him, and he'd notice the guttering, and the moss beginning to peek through the patio cracks. She would become yet another thing for him to fit into his week. She did not want this or the alternative which was a fold or moving in with one of them. She made a note in her head to ask the minister's advice. He was impartial and it would give her a diversion – something else to talk about – when she felt him lumbering up for prayer.

The young minister remained just as faithful as ever. He came to visit every Tuesday en route to the senior citizens' lunch. By the third week of widowhood, these pastoral visits had fallen into a pale routine. Tea was taken, sometimes with cake or chocolate biscuits. Then they made general conversation about people they knew and things which had recently happened, mostly in the East. Sandra enjoyed these chats. She looked forward to them. The minister was a fine storyteller. He could bring the city right into her living room so, for a short hour, she did not feel quite so removed from the streets outside her front door.

However, these visits were not without purpose. Every act, including the particular way he sat on the sofa's edge, neither absent nor fully committed, was a mere preamble to the praying. Once his teacup had been drained and topped up and drained again, the young minister would set it, quite deliberately, on the carpet by his feet. Adjusting his trousers at the thigh, his voice would make the barely perceivable slide from secular to spiritual. Like all good clergymen, the Reverend Cunningham kept a second, slightly forced, accent for talking to and about God. It helped Sandra to imagine this process as a key change, like Boyzone or one of those other bands of young lads going up an octave every time they hit a bridge. However, the young minister's voice did not rise. It descended: down, down, down to the carpet and the heels of his well-polished brogues. 'Well,' he'd say holding his own hand in his lap, as if it did not belong to him, 'how's it been this week, Sandra?' The 'it' was not her health or even her grief, but rather some ill-defined place between faith and unbelief, an island of sorts, perpetually adrift.

'It's not easy, Mr Cunningham,' she'd say. 'It's not easy at all. I want to believe God's up there and he's listening. But I don't feel anything any more.'

'Feelings come and go,' the young minister would answer quickly, 'and God isn't the least bit affected by how you feel about him. He's still there Sandra, no matter what you believe. There's far too much talk about feelings these days. Proper faith is believing in things you can't see or feel.'

'I suppose you're right,' Sandra agreed. She did not see the sense in devoting herself to something which couldn't be depended upon. Jim's faith had been a blanket, big enough for both of them. Without him, it was hard to remember if she'd ever really believed at all.

At the beginning of April, Sandra noticed the crocuses. Jim had planted them himself, filling the plastic planters which ran the length of their windowsills with handfuls of onion-coloured bulbs. 'They were in a box in the shed,' he'd said. 'I've no idea what they are, maybe snowdrops or miniature daffodils. Sure, we'll see in the spring, when they come up.' He'd never been much of a gardener – more of a handyman – but the crocuses tore into Sandra every time she drew the curtains back. She could picture him with a trowel and the particular hat he'd kept for gardening. She let the crocuses be, relishing the way they crept along her windowsill like a slow bruise. Their heads, by the second week, had already started to hang and nosed at the soil as if ashamed of their own beauty.

'Is it Easter soon?' she asked her son on the telephone.

'Next week,' he replied and Sandra said that she'd thought as much, on account of the crocuses and the nights growing longer.

'Will you come to us for Easter, Mum?' he asked, and she said she was looking forward to it. This was neither a lie, nor the truth entirely.

She asked how many days it was to Easter. It was nine; just a little over a week. This seemed believable. She made a note in her head of the number and planned to write it down once her son had hung up.

She asked if the weans would be better off with money

instead of Easter eggs, and her son said either would be fine and she really didn't have to bother this year, on account of Jim.

She thought, without saying it, that Easter would be a line under all this ugliness.

For weeks, Sandra had been bracing herself for Easter.

Lent was always a thin time. Even during ordinary years, she'd kept herself half starved right through till the last Sunday. It was how she'd been brought up, how she'd raised her own three children. 'You give things up,' she'd taught them, as soon as they were old enough to understand, 'and it's hard. Don't let anyone tell you it's not. But the missing makes you lean all the more on the Lord. Lent's there to show God you're serious about him.'

When the children were really young, before they'd made professions of their own, she'd made the decision for them. Emptying her larder of all but the staples, she'd fed them three bland meals a day and plain digestives when they asked for something after dinner. She hoped they had understood the difference between sacrifice and punishment. She was never quite sure if she entirely understood herself. She'd been harder on the children than Jim, who'd slipped them creme eggs when Sandra wasn't looking, and let them read comics in church during the sermon. Jim, whose belief had remained as wide as the transatlantic gulf and had not required proof nor testing of any sort.

Sandra had loved the quiet faith in her husband and also envied him. Occasionally, catching his eye over the Communion cup, she'd seen a loud, white belief slip over him. He shone like Jesus in the children's illustrated Bible. In these honest moments, she could not have despised him more.

She would starve herself during Lent and still feel further from God with each small sacrifice. Lent, for Sandra, had been nothing to do with leaning. Lent was only ever anticipating the moment when everything would be returned to her: chocolate and daytime television, Nivea moisturiser and the joy of the Lord's presence, which was sometimes difficult to distinguish from the pleasure of a finally full belly.

For forty days, Sandra's God would be dead. She'd press hard into the hunger surrounding his absence, enjoying the way it twisted inside her. This had nothing to do with holiness. It was teeth. It was physical like the need for bread, or sometimes, after eating bacon, a Coca Cola, like the times she'd kept herself from Jim before and after the children, too sore to allow him close, too raw to bear his absence.

For forty days, Sandra would feel lonely for God. Though she could not admit it to herself, this dry lust was the only thing which separated her from her unbelieving neighbours, who smoked and sexed widely, and got their groceries in on a Sunday afternoon.

Easter morning had always been a relief for her. Between the flowers and the children and the up-from-the-grave-he-arose triumphalism, there was no room for doubt, either general or specific. 'He is risen indeed,' she would repeat silently, testing each word for its breaking point. She'd keep her eye on the place where the paint had peeled off in the shape of a bird. Her lips would never move. And, with this unspoken confession, Sandra had permitted herself another year of demure belief. God had been returned unto her unbroken, and all the lesser joys would come sloping after.

This year would be different. Even Easter could not bring Jim back to her. Sandra's God was not brazen; he was no longer in the habit of miracles. Yet, she expected to receive something in return for her loss: a glimpse of his purpose or a moment of the resting peace so many people had written about inside their sympathy cards. She believed that Easter morning would bring an end to God's silence. After Easter they would begin again, with bruises, like a couple committing to give it one more painful try.

On Easter Sunday, Sandra felt no different than she had the previous day, which had been a Saturday with rain and a fish supper for tea. She sat in the pew between her son and Sam. The child was not used to sitting through a whole church service and could not keep his boredom still. Sandra was glad of the distraction. She fed him Polo mints and dandered him on her knee. Looking down the side of her grandson, she did not have to confront her disappointment directly.

'Gran, it's Easter,' the boy said. 'Jesus died on the cross today.'

'That was Friday,' she whispered. 'It's Sunday now. He's not dead any more.'

'Why's he not here then?' Sam asked. Sandra had no good answer for the boy so she opened a second packet of Polo mints and passed them to him two at a time. He crunched them noisily, opening and closing his mouth so she could see the white shards on his tongue like tiny splinters of bone or tooth.

During the service, three young people were baptised on profession of faith. Baptisms were a new thing for Easter morning. The young minister had introduced them a few years back, not just for babies, for adults too. Baptisms were the perfect way to celebrate the Easter resurrection. 'Such a joy, to see these three dear children choosing today to enter into Christ's death and resurrection,' the young minister began. 'Yet another reason to celebrate on Easter Sunday morning. Aren't we blessed folks? Isn't God immeasurably good?'

The new believers lined up beside the baptismal font to share their testimonies and take a blessing. As they bowed their heads to receive a teaspoonful of water from the minister's hand – three almost-grown adults in suits and heels – the urge to laugh came rushing up Sandra's throat like a demon thing she had not known or nurtured. 'You fools!' she wanted to cry out. 'You lost, lost fools!'

The sun was rushing through the stained-glass window of Noah's ark, turning the tops of their heads rainbow-coloured in stripes. They were like heavenly beings or Christmas lights blinking at the front of the church. The verse, 'and I will remember my covenant which is between me and you', rose up within her, God's promise after the Flood. The words had never held for Sandra and they did not hold now. She was too proud or stubborn, too bound to those truths you could prove with your eyes or your holding hands. These three, sleek-haired youngsters were believing as she had never been able to believe herself.

She glanced to her left and right, to the pew in front where all her close friends and family had gathered like soldiers swarming around a fallen comrade. They were light with the belief that everything, even this, had a purpose. They could have been glowing. Sandra was heavy and always standing to the side of their joy. She felt herself warming with jealousy, sweat collecting at the base of her spine and behind her knees. She knew that when she rose for the next hymn, there'd be a damp perspiration patch left in the pew behind her, and she could not control her own heat.

That evening, after the roast had been eaten and the table cleared in preparation for a new week, Sandra read the grandchildren their bedtime stories. Horse books for the girls, and for Sam, who slept in his own bunked bedroom, a picture book about aliens with brightly coloured pictures. She tucked him in tightly, drawing the duvet up to the child's chin so his head seemed severed from the thin, pyjama-clad body curled beneath the blankets. His breath, when she bent to kiss him, was minted; chalk-white toothpaste crusted in the corners of his mouth. He slept with a plastic action figure now – Buzz Lightyear or Spiderman – already too old for teddy bears.

'Will you do my prayers, Gran?' he asked.

There was no room for distraction in such a tiny space. The walls inched just a little closer to Sandra, the ceiling seemed inclined to fall, and, grasping the rails of Sammy's bunk bed, she felt her lungs struggle to stay afloat. She had not the strength to manage this today.

'It's late, Sammy,' she replied, trying to keep her voice a straight, measured line, 'and you've had a really long day.'

'Mummy and Daddy always do my prayers before I go to sleep.'

So Sandra prayed with the child. She put words together to make sentences, simple sentences she'd probably said a hundred times or more. She spoke them over him in a praying voice and kept her eyes closed. She could not bear to look at her grandson while lying. She would tell this lie for the rest of her life, to Sammy and other people she loved. She'd never be able to bring herself to hurt them.

Outside in the hall, she leant against the closed bathroom door and tried to pray, 'Lord have mercy on me, a sinner.' She allowed her lips to move over the words but no noise came out. 'Lord have mercy on me, a sinner.' Even this, the simplest of all prayers, seemed stuck inside her like a tumour too far gone. 'Lord have mercy on me, a sinner.' It wasn't even a thing that proper Protestants said. She gave up and went downstairs to put the kettle on. As she passed his bedroom door, Sandra could hear Sam singing to himself in the dark, his voice fumbling around the words of a popular Sunday-school chorus. This was almost too much to carry alone.

15.
Children's Children

They met, by arrangement, at the rock that looked like a rabbit from one side and the Empire State Building from the other. She had never ventured further north and knew it only as a rabbit. He knew nothing of the south. The rock had been a skyscraper to him for as long as he could remember.

She was the last and he was the last. All the other young ones had left for the mainland with the notion of becoming beauty therapists or PhD students. The pair of them were leftover children, too fat and faithful to consider leaving. They did not dream remembering dreams, nor indulge themselves in ambition. They felt physically ill if they went so much as a single day without encountering the ocean. They knew nothing more than the placid seasons of their parents and grandparents: up with the sun, down with the cows, and television for all those needs which could not be grown, or hauled – sleek gilled and flappering – from the sea.

They were leftover children, set aside for such a time as this. Tomorrow they would be married for the good of the island, both northern and southern sides. They understood what this meant and could picture themselves tomorrow evening, in good clothes, with music. Yet, when they tried to imagine one month later, drinking tea and making up a stranger's bed, they could not alight upon anything more concrete than the details: shoelaces, crockery, the caustic smell of Lifebuoy soap on an unfamiliar sink.

They understood entirely but had not been given a choice. The arrangement was a simple mathematical equation; if more people were not soonly made, there would be no one left to keep the island afloat. They would marry for the good of everyone, themselves included. Little thought had been given to what would happen after their marrying. Questions such as which side of the island they might settle on, or who their children would marry, or where they would eat their Christmas dinner when Christmas made its annual appearance, had not been considered.

The rock marked the exact midpoint of the island, seven foresty miles from the northern shore and a similar, open-fielded seven from the opposite coastline. The island was long and puckered like a section of intestine, recently unravelled. It was drenched in the winter and barely dry by the time summer had folded into autumn. Each year it lost ten to twenty stones of weight as, one by one, and occasionally in couples, the young ones caught the ferry to the mainland and never returned. Bolstered by this newfound lightness the island's tideline had receded by three centimetres in the last decade. This extra pinch of pebbly sand was widely attributed to global warming. The islanders rested easy, convinced that they, and they alone, were riding high while the rest of the world sunk on the whim of a polar icecap.

The islanders were a staunch and meaty breed, shock-haired, handsome and raised on short-loan classics from the library boat which visited once a month on a Wednesday. They lived in either the north or the south. Even those who hovered around the midlands, like small children toeing the bonfire's edge, knew exactly which side of the line they laid their heads on. On the island you were north or you were south, or you left for the mainland. The east and west were not to be considered. They remained geographical afterthoughts, as inconsequential as a pair of open brackets. Once, in the 1970s, a half mile of the east coast had unhooked itself and floated off to Lanzarote or some such sunny place. No one had noticed or particularly cared, for the peripheral directions had remained unimportant so long as north had stayed north and south had continued to dominate the southern extremities.

All the island's children had been formed from the same sandy soil and sprouted annually, in metric units, towards the same sap-grey sky. They spoke the same words, darkly set, and drunk from the same slow river, rising as it did in the north, and fumbling southwards through fields and forests in pursuit of the motherless ocean. When it rained, as it every day did, it was the same cloud sulk which settled on all their pitched roofs, their swing sets and off-road vehicles, the same rain which coaxed the lazy turnips out of the island's muck-thick belly and into their soup pots.

The people were consistent as common spades, on either side of the border. Yet, it was unheard of to point these similarities out to an islander currently resident. In 1973, a young fella who'd come to make a documentary film had been drowned by the feet and posted home in envelopes for claiming it was sheer stupidity to split the island while the same sort of people lived on either side of the border. The islanders could not so much as look in a puddle for noting just how different they were from their neighbours across the border. They prided themselves on variegated eyebrows, specialist cuisine and sporting activities peculiar to their own backyards. Even a throwaway comment from a visiting mainlander, such as, 'Do all the good folk on this island have the same lovely shade of hair?' or 'Youse ones on the island are fairly good at the old boatbuilding, are you not?' could turn an islander purple with indignation. No true southerner wished to be mistaken for an eejit from the north. Neither did the northerners wish to exhibit habits or haircuts distinctly associated with the south.

As she approached the rock, she recognised him. He was shorter than his photograph but the moustache was familiar, also the furious eyebrows. And, if she was not greatly mistaken he was wearing the same faded polo shirt he'd worn the day his picture had been taken.

He'd never seen her before, in person or print, but as she was the only woman in a field of trees, rocks and twitchetty sheep, he rightly assumed her to be his wife.

'Are you she?' he asked.

She nodded. Her hat crept up her forehead and came to rest like a dollop of cream on the peak of her crown. She was pretty enough, like a lady on local television, but not the sort you'd see in the movies.

'Are you he?' she asked.

'I am for sure,' he replied.

The sound of him was all through his nose and strained, exactly like her Uncle Mikey from the north, who she'd only heard on the telephone and once in person, as a small child, at her grandmother's funeral.

'I brought sandwiches,' she said, and he wondered if they put the same things in their sandwiches on the other side of the island.

He'd heard from his brother Paul, who lived on the mainland now, that they buttered their sandwiches with mayonnaise in the south. This was probably just rumouring though. Ever since the island had split in two, like a pair of book pages parting, all sorts of stories had crept backwards and forwards across the border:

the northerners kept their old ones in with the chickens; the folks of the south did not believe in dentists or even toothbrushes; they had not yet got satellite television or even microwave ovens in the north. As children they'd passed these rumours round the primary playground, gently, gently with cupped hands and low-ered voices. They were too old for such nonsense by the time they arrived at big school. Big school was a Portakabin in the corner of the primary playground, with proper-sized toilets and a set of encyclopaedias preaching leather-bound reason from the topmost shelf of the bookcase. In light of histories as definite as Martin Luther King, the Battle of Hastings and also the Holo-caust, it was ludicrous to believe sheer fluff and speculation. Yet the rumours were too delicious to let go of entirely.

'Here,' she said, 'have a ham sandwich.'

She unpeeled the tinfoil for him and passed the naked sand-wich across the border. They sat down on the grass. She on her side, he on his. He pressed the two pieces of bread together and mayonnaise oozed out between the crusts.

'There's mayonnaise on this here sandwich,' he cried. 'Are youse mad over there in the south?'

'Youse can talk, putting red sauce in your tea; most disgusting thing I ever heard.'

'We do not.' But there was no way of proving this without a teapot.

They ate their sandwiches in silence. The mayonnaise nearly made him boke but he didn't want to put her off before they were even married. She watched him eating. The way the saliva caught in the corners of his mouth, like cuckoo spit stretching with every bite, turned her stomach. She was not used to people eating with such animal enthusiasm but she tried not to stare. When they were married she would start into his manners, teach him how civilised people approached an eating table.

'So, are you up for this then?' he asked.

'I suppose so.'

'Happy enough with what you're getting?'

'I'm sure you're in the same boat as me. I'd always planned on wedding one of our sort.'

'Desperate times, eh?'

'Are you saying I'm ugly?'

'Course not, sweetheart. You're definitely not the worst-looking woman on this island. It's just, I think neither of us would be doing this if there was anybody left on our own side.'

'Anybody else at all.'

'Still it's for the good of the island isn't it? We've to make a wee sacrifice for the auld ones.'

'We do indeed, sure haven't they always put us first?'

They fell to talking, he and then she, describing at length the very many exotic things which existed on their sides of the island: tall trees in the north and a man with seven fingers in the south, five kinds of ale on her side of the line and five completely different, but similarly potent, draughts on his.

The sound of him was a Continental holiday against the boredom. She found herself goosebumpling up and down her forearms, much afraid and also excited.

The sound of her was a shotgun far away and not quite threatening.

They were all but ready to cross the border, to skip the priests and get on with the good act of marrying, when the future sneaked out like a stifled fart.

'Your side or mine?' he asked.

She feigned grace and offered to move north for the sake of her husband's kin. (This was a lie of sorts, lovingly told and masking her desire to live, for the first time beneath trees, with foxes, in the company of singing folk.) He countered her lies with his own. He would move south, first for the good of his wife, then for the prospect of open fields and fresh milk and the lion's slice of morning sun.

They could not settle upon a side, for the land changed shape the moment you crossed the border. Ten minutes before their wedding day they realised that the island was asking more of them than they could ever manage.

'If we both move north, we'll upset the balance and tip the island into the sea,' he explained, holding her little hand coldly across the border.

'And if we settle in the south, things will be skewed in that direction,' she cried, 'never mind what'll happen when we start having the weans.'

'The weight of us combined could ruin everything.'

They unclasped, hands coming apart like two ends of an ancient necklace. She sat cross-legged in the south and he watched the dawn descend upon the northern face of the rock. They held their silence reverently and wondered if they loved the island enough to be neither north nor south, foreigner or familiar, but rather a brave new direction, balanced like a hairline fracture in the centre of everything.

Notes

'We've Got Each Other and That's a Lot' was longlisted for the Sean O'Faoloin Prize 2015

'Still' was published in *Elbow Room* 2015

'Children's Children' was published in The Curfew Tower Is Many Things 2015

'Shopping' was published in *The Incubator* in 2014

'Alternative Uses for a Belfast Box Room' was published in *The Honest Ulsterman* in 2014

'More of a Handstand Girl' was published in *Storm Cellar* in 2014

Also by Jan Carson

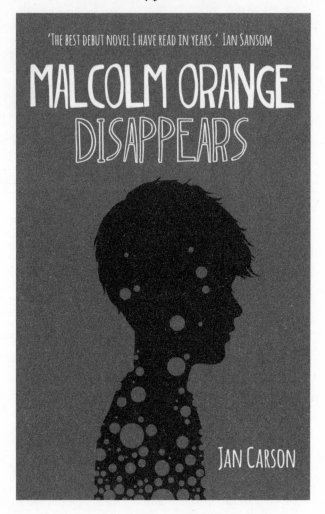

'A born storyteller, [Carson's] narratives are uncontainable, fizzing up out of her pages like soda and vinegar in a bottle.' —*Guardian*

'At its best, *Malcolm Orange Disappear*s reminds the reader of Kurt Vonnegut and other masters of the absurd – Carson can be very, very funny. All of Carson's touches of magic realism are perfectly judged.' —*Sunday Business Post*

'A highly original book; very quirky.' —*Irish Examiner*